Ground Static

Lyra Xolani

Published by Lyra Xolani, 2025.

GROUND STATIC

First edition. May 14, 2025.

Copyright © 2025 Lyra Xolani.

ISBN: 979-8998929618

Written by Lyra Xolani.

This book is dedicated to my family and to the diaspora in the present and future.

Chapter 1: Ground Static & Resonance

Keket

The gut feeling hit first. Sharp. Unsettling. Weeks spent poring over grainy preliminary drone scans in the isolation of a deep-space lab. The Ganymede Prime Silicates —a unique silicate structure that promised breakthroughs: hyperefficient atmospheric processors, clean water for struggling colonies, maybe even a significant boost for the Sanction's ambitious terraforming project back home. Proof that exploration, real exploration pushing the boundaries of the known, mattered more than profit margins. My Watcher's intuition, a legacy rooted in the old ways of Ma'at, screamed significance, pulling me towards subtle anomalies others had dismissed as environmental noise. There was a genuine thrill in the discovery, a desperate need for something real. Something vital. And perhaps, though I rarely let the thought surface, a connection just as real. My work, while vital, was a solitary pursuit, the hum of the lab her only constant companion. The Watcher legacy spoke of perceiving unseen currents, but what of the currents that might bind one soul to another? Such thoughts were unproductive, a distraction from the precise data before me, yet they flickered sometimes, in the quiet hours between scans, a faint, undefined ache for a resonance beyond the scientific.

Instead, OmniCorp Energy —Mom's domain, that monolithic corporate titan with its ubiquitous, ironically stylized Eye of Horus logo promising foresight and prosperity —had seized it. Their legal teams. Their resource acquisition specialists. They had moved with ruthless efficiency, locking down the patent, burying the research under layers of proprietary code, deemed too valuable for public distribution. Now, that revolutionary material adorned luxury RTV-7 filtration tech. State-of-the-art purifiers marketed for penthouse suites in orbital pleasure habitats and private yachts cruising through the asteroid belt. Their polished hulls reflecting the indifferent void. A sharp, cold image flashed behind my eyes, triggered by the sheer audacity of the corporate emblem: the dull, vacant eyes of a child struggling for breath behind a cracked atmospheric filter. A memory from the Cerulean Plaque outbreak season, just three years ago. The lower hab-levels, crammed with people deemed non-essential or lacking sufficient credits, had choked on air thick with

1

airborne pathogens. The thin, desperate sound of ragged, rasping coughs. The contrast was a physical blow. A nauseating counterpoint to the station's relentless, indifferent hum. I could still almost taste the acrid, sickness-sweet smell that had clung to the lower hab med-bay during the worst of it. Thick with fear and fever and the metallic tang of inadequate filtration. A stark reminder of who truly paid the price for "strategic resource allocation".

"Strategic resource allocation," Mom had called it. Clipped. Dismissive. A comm call. Her face projected, efficient, slightly blurred by interstellar static. Her focus already elsewhere. How could I reconcile that sickening hypocrisy, that calculated cruelty masked as efficiency, with signing off on reports optimizing extraction routes for PetroMax Interstellar? Dad's employer. OmniCorp's equally vast and voracious counterpart in the relentless consumption of planetary resources. Each approved plan felt like another rivet hammered into the hull of the very system I despised. A relentless engine of profit that saw planets as quarries to be hollowed out and people as acceptable losses in the pursuit of growth. As an ad-drone glided past, its synthetic voice blaring PetroMax's slogan in the hub's transit corridors, "Powering the Future", my hand clenched involuntarily over the console. The cool plasti-alloy was a poor substitute for the visceral anger tightening in my gut. Whose future, exactly? Not the child in my memory. That was certain.

Another rotation cycle bled into the next aboard this sterile processing hub orbiting Earth. Each hour here felt like a flat, colorless echo of the last. The low hum of Orbital Command Station Epsilon was a constant, monotonous vibration. It sank into the deck plates, a physical reminder of the station's immense, impersonal power. A reminder of my own minuscule, equally impersonal role within its machinery. My gaze was fixed on the cascading data streams – rivers of glowing green and amber digits, endless lines of clean code. They represented mineral yields from distant moons, projected energy needs for system colonies, logistical optimizations for distribution networks. Below the pristine data, I knew the sub-feeds hinted at the truth: rationing on Cygnus X-1 Prime, civil unrest brewing on the Kepler settlements – the cost of an empire built on spreadsheets. I thought of Jian, the contact I had there, waiting on supplies that might never arrive. The clean, efficient logic of it all felt utterly, soul-crushingly unsatisfying. A hollow hum against the persistent ache of restlessness. It tightened my chest, made my fingers twitch over the console.

The recycled air tasted flat, metallic, devoid of life or scent, like the reports piling up for my approval. Efficient. Necessary. Ultimately hollow.

This intricate dance of logistics and hyperspace jumps, this service to the Sah Collective that saw itself as the benevolent steward of humanity's expansion among the stars, was the family business. It was tied to the 'Watcher' legacy – that ancestral knack for deep-field acuity, a sensitivity to the subtle energies of spacetime and planetary fields, the ability to perceive the unseen currents. Nana always told me it was rooted in the old ways of Ma'at, of perceiving the universe's underlying balance. Not just through what the eyes could see, or the sensors could register, but through instinct. By resonating with cosmic currents. She'd speak of priestesses charting the stars by the whispers of the wind and the alignment of constellations, their wisdom passed down through generations, echoing the Griots of old Earth who carried history and guidance in their voices, shaping narratives not just for entertainment, but for survival. I'd heard whispers too, of others in our line, some who vanished into the void, others who chose paths far from the Collective's eye. Tech augmentation – the bio-filaments and neural interfaces – sharpened it. Quantified it. Turned it into a marketable skill the Collective eagerly sought out as easily accessible resources dwindled. These integrated systems didn't just enhance natural perception; they translated the subtle energies Keket's lineage sensed – shifts in spacetime, planetary fields, resonant frequencies – into quantifiable data streams and sensory input her conscious mind could interpret and interact with. Turning instinct into a powerful, technological tool. But the core of it, the Ashe flowing through our line, the intuitive understanding, was something older. Something OmniCorp couldn't synthesize or patent. Something that resisted quantification. And that's what made us valuable assets in this system, sought after by the very powers I resented. As I navigated complex interface controls, my fingers tracing elegant curves on the holographic display – symbols echoing ancient Kemetic glyphs for 'journey' and 'sky,' overlaid onto standard Collective astrogation data – it felt less like cold calculation and more like breathing. The symbols flowed naturally under my touch. This inherent connection, amplified by technology, was my strength. But also the chain that bound me.

My gaze drifted past the data streams towards the viewport. A momentary escape from the digital cage. Below, Earth turned slowly. A scarred blue-green marble veiled by swirling clouds. The faint, intricate shimmer of the defense grid that encased its atmosphere. It was a view I'd known since childhood visits to my parents' duty stations – a familiar backdrop. A reminder of where we came from, the cradle of humanity. But not a place I truly considered home anymore. That anchor, if I had one, was the star-dusted void that stretched endlessly beyond, dotted with the distant light of colonized systems. The promise of the unknown. Out there, barely visible under the atmospheric haze and beyond the hub's climate-controlled environment, beyond the immediate, suffocating reach of corporate tentacles (or so I desperately hoped), was the North East Coast Sanction. My Sanction. A sprawling mecca of African American innovation on old Earth. A collective gamble in a different way, pinning hope on collaboration instead of exploitation, on building something sustainable and equitable outside the dominant, extractive model. It was supposed to be different. I clung to that hope. A fragile ember in the constant wind of my cynicism, even as my current task demanded I feed the machine working against it.

Restlessness pulsed under my skin. A kinetic energy that had no outlet here. Only the hub's sterile efficiency. I wanted dirt under my fingernails. The unpredictable thrill of discovery. The challenge of the unknown. The raw, unfiltered data of an alien world – not this endless cycle of optimizing exploitation from a climate-controlled cage high above the world. I wanted my work to mean something. To build. To contribute something real, not just extract value for the benefit of a few. The desire was a physical ache. A yearning for escape velocity from this gilded prison of data and complicity. Which was precisely why I felt this restless energy now, hours before my scheduled Perception Calibration. I needed Command's sterile focus, the rigorous mental discipline honed by years of deep-space navigation. To push down the cynicism. To access the professional core required for whatever was coming. The vastness of space outside was somewhat offset by the floor-to-ceiling murals depicting star lanes in vibrant geometric patterns of old Ghanaian Kente cloth – a splash of defiant color mandated by the Diaspora Accords, a hard-won treaty after the Scattering that aimed to preserve cultural identity and history across the stars. A reminder that even in the void, our past journeyed with us. I traced the lines with my gaze. Each sharp angle and flowing curve telling a story whispered across lightyears. The deep blues spoke of vast distances. The fiery oranges of newborn suns. The earth browns, a reminder of the house we left behind. It was beautiful, yes, a vital link to a fragmented past. But tonight, even their beauty felt... hollow. Another artifact in a life that felt increasingly detached.

This wasn't routine. The Collective didn't schedule full-spectrum Calibrations, honing my Watcher acuity to its absolute peak, amplifying that innate ability to perceive the subtle energies of spacetime and planetary fields, without significant reason. Whispers had been circulating through the secure channels. Hushed reports speaking of a critical resource need – something vital for the next-gen Phase-Channel conduits underpinning all faster-than-light interstellar travel. Stabilizing those conduits meant relieving pressure on the overburdened hyperlane network, which was nearing breaking point. Allowing sustainable settlement of developing colonies. Not just frantic, unsustainable expansion driven by dwindling resources. Across the galaxy, supply lines were stretching thin. Colonies were facing resource shortages. The fragile peace of the Collective's expansion was threatened. This wasn't just a future problem. It was a crisis point now. A goal even my cynical side admitted held genuine merit beyond simple corporate or Collective profit. And tasks requiring this level of sensory enhancement, navigating hazardous, data-rich environments that would overload standard sensors ... they fell by necessity to those with the innate acuity, amplified by technology. The 'Watcher' lineage. My legacy. My marketable skill. My inescapable responsibility.

A clipped comm pinged. This time a direct priority channel overriding routine traffic. Mom's face flickered onto my display. Her brow furrowed with that familiar work-induced stress. "Keket, status report on the Eridani survey due tomorrow. Corporate wants those projections finalized." The routine demands of the machine. Always pressing. "Almost done, Mom," I replied, forcing a professional tone. "Just running the final simulations." "Good. PetroMax needs those jump coordinates by 0800. Your Dad's waiting on them." The constant pressure. The endless deadlines. And then, the static truly set in. "Love you, Keket," she said, her voice a little strained. Her eyes already drifting back to the data streams. "Love you too," I murmured to the empty air after the connection severed. Ghosts in the machine. Some days, living felt like waiting in a beautifully engineered dead end. The console screen returned to my task list, highlighting the next step in the PetroMax reports. My finger hovered over the approval key. Hesitating. That sick feeling twisted in my gut again. But before I could dwell on the bitter taste of compromise, a sharp, system-wide alert overrode my console's soft hum. Cutting through the ambient noise. A priority signal. Classified. My screen blanked. Then resolved into the face of Anya Sharma, Prime Coordinator of the Sah Collective. Her presence cut through the lingering static of the call and the weight of my own thoughts. Her face was composed, as always. But her eyes were sharp, assessing me with that unnerving intensity. "Keket," her voice was crisp, efficient, leaving no room for ambiguity. "Your Perception Calibration is scheduled post-rotation, correct? Commander Jian confirms readiness at the Sensory Integration Suite." "Confirmed, Prime Coordinator. Systems nominal. I am prepared." I kept my tone equally professional, recognizing the shift in focus from corporate demands to Collective necessity. "Excellent." Sharma's gaze sharpened further, and a hint of something unreadable, a spark of urgency that cut through her usual calm, flashed in her eyes. This wasn't just a routine check. This was the reason for the high-level calibration, the whispers of critical need solidified into a direct order. "Because we have an assignment requiring your specific skill set immediately following. Designation: Xylos, uninhabited terrestrial world, Gliese 581 system."

The standard star chart dissolved instantly, replaced by telemetry on a swirling emerald sphere that filled the screen. It pulsed with an almost unsettling energy. Vibrant and alive even on the flat display, unlike the dead data I usually worked with. "Preliminary scans indicate significant Scarabite-7 deposits," Sharma continued, her voice picking up a note of urgency as she zoomed in on jagged energy spikes emanating from the planet's surface. "More importantly, these deposits exhibit unusual phase-resonant properties crucial for stabilizing next-gen Phase-Channel conduits. Our hyperlane network nears capacity, Keket. Without stable conduits from Scarabite-7, supply to developing colonies like Cygnus X-1 Prime bottlenecks catastrophically within five cycles." The projected reality wasn't just hardship. It was starvation. Civil unrest. The projections are grim. The Collective needs this. Desperately. And that desperation meant they might not be patient or diplomatic.

Unusual phase-resonant properties... It reminded me of fragmented historical data on this system, mentioning indigenous legends. My enhanced senses, even uncalibrated, felt a subtle wrongness on the telemetry. Unstable tectonic harmonics. Significant bio-resonant cascades. And the planet's core energy readings showed immense power. But also a strange, rhythmic modulation. A pulse that felt less like a geological process and more like a conscious beat, resonating on frequencies my Watcher senses instinctively recognized as 'aligned'. Among the fragmented historical data, I recalled indigenous warnings regarding 'unraveling light' and 'currents that bite' – dismissed as primitive superstition. But now, facing the reality of Xylos, the phrases felt chillingly specific. "The challenge," Sharma elaborated, highlighting anomalous readings clustered specifically around the Scarabite-7 deposits. "Lies in the environment. Xylos presents... irregularities. Standard automated extraction is high-risk, potentially catastrophic to automated systems attempting to process such volatile energy signatures." Her gaze met mine across the distance, direct and unwavering. "We need direct assessment, Keket. Human analysis, guided by enhanced perception. Your acuity... is paramount for navigating safely and identifying stable extraction points. Automated systems cannot replicate the nuance of Watcher perception." Anya gestured to the swirling green image. "This isn't just resource acquisition, Keket. It's navigating the unknown under hazardous conditions. A true frontier task. Xylos is key to the Collective's – and by extension, Diaspora's, the Sanction, all our scattered worlds' – immediate future stability." The pull was undeniable. The allure of the unknown. The challenge that demanded everything my unique heritage and training had prepared me for. The anomalous readings sparked my professional curiosity. Not heritage as some mystical claim, but as a foundation for a practical capability the Collective desperately needed for this specific, challenging environment. Staring into the star-dusted void beyond the viewport – always more like home than Earth – the familiar pull of the unknown warred with a weariness I rarely allowed myself to acknowledge. The emerald dream of untouched worlds lingered. Time to prepare. This calibration wasn't a general power-up; it was the crucial step in attuning my senses to the specific, volatile energies of Xylos, the only way to safely navigate the anomalies Sharma described and locate the vital Scarabite-7. My journey, defined not just by ancestors and their ancient wisdom, but by where my skills could take me, by the mysteries I could unravel, was truly beginning. It began here, preparing specifically for the unknown pulse and vibrant chaos of Xylos.

Chapter 2: Sensory Calibration for the Emerald World

Keket

Later that day, the Sensory Integration Suite was a sanctuary of quiet. A stark contrast to the bustling energy of Command. A stark contrast to the constant hum of the processing hub. It was designed as a harmonious, zen-like space, drawing inspiration from Feng Shui principles. To promote focus. To promote receptivity. To quiet the external noise and allow the internal senses to come to the fore. Soft, diffused light bathed the room, filtering through climbing plants that cascaded down a living wall. Their leaves were a vibrant, calming green. A gentle waterfall trickled down the center of that wall. Its soothing sound mingled with the low, almost imperceptible hum of the station's deeper systems. A sound I was about to become intimately familiar with. The minimalist room centered around a reclined chair. Sleek and ergonomic. The walls were adorned with murals of calming greens and blues, abstract patterns that seemed to flow and shift. Designed to soothe. Designed to prepare the mind. It wasn't a chamber of whispers or sterile machinery, not like the medical bays or the engine core. It was a lab. Meticulously designed for honing human senses. Pushing them beyond their natural limits.

Anya Sharma, the lead mind behind the neuro-sensory program – her lineage tracing back to those who first translated 'Watcher' intuition into quantifiable cognitive science – oversaw my final calibration. She wasn't the crisp, authoritative Coordinator now. She was the focused expert. Her silver hair tied back tight. Her eyes sharp and assessing as she reviewed diagnostics on a handheld pad. Confirming everything was within parameters. There was a quiet intensity to her. A deep understanding of the intricate systems she worked with. But also a hint of warmth. A reassuring presence that cut through my apprehension.

"Lie back, Keket," she instructed calmly. Her voice gentle. A calming presence in quiet space. I settled into the chair. The cool, smooth material is a welcome contrast to my own warm skin. Adjusting my position, mindful of my height. My long locs brushing softly against the headrest. A familiar faint blue glow emanated from the tattoos tracing intricate paths from beside my ear, down my neck and shoulder, onto my arm. Visible even in the soft light. Visible manifestation of my bio-integrated systems. The tech woven with my biology. I met Anya's gaze with my own. Steadying my breath. Ready for the process to begin.

"Vitals optimal. Xylos's unique and complex interference signatures necessitate full-spectrum enhancement," Anya stated. Her voice steady and professional. Confirming the explicit need for *this level* of advanced calibration, linking it directly to the planet awaiting me.

Articulated arms tipped with micro-emitters moved with precise, near-surgical grace around my forearms and temples. Positioning themselves with uncanny accuracy. I felt precise, near-painless tingles as the microscopic pathways of the bio-filaments snaked beneath my skin. Branching from enhanced nerve bundles. Interfacing directly with my peripheral nervous system. Amplifying specific sensory inputs. Preparing me to perceive the world in ways few others could. They pulsed with a soft, internal light. Intricate patterns like glowing veins beneath my skin. Mirroring the visible tattoos. A lightweight neural interface headset, cool and smooth against my skin, lowered over my eyes and ears. Sealing me in a world of controlled input.

"Beginning with somatic amplification," Anya stated, her voice a soothing presence through the headset's internal speakers. "Xylos's unstable tectonic harmonics and bio-resonant cascades are primary concerns. This network lets you perceive subsonic frequencies, micro-vibrations *below standard thresholds*. Subtle tremors to the planet itself. Feel geological stress shifts before they become critical. Sense the planet's deep pulse." A low hum filled my awareness. Not as the sound my ears perceive. As a vibration resonating through the station's structure. Through the chair. Into my very bones. Data my conscious mind never registered before. The deep, underlying pulse of the station. Soon to be replaced by the pulse of a world. It was a subtle tremor on the floor. A faint pulse in the walls. A new layer of reality is opening. This specific somatic tuning was vital. Xylos wasn't just geologically active; Sharma's briefing mentioned *unstable* harmonics. Detecting those micro-vibrations early could mean the difference between navigating a fissure and being swallowed by one.

"Next, chemo-reception enhancement. Targeted catalysts heighten olfactory and gustatory sensitivity and pattern recognition. Identify trace chemical signatures and vectors instantly, given the atmospheric cascades and potential biological contaminants on Xylos." The sterile air around me resolved into its component parts. No longer flat and metallic. The sharp tang of ozone from the station's systems. The metallic trace from the ventilation system. The subtle scent of the chair's polymers. The faint, clean smell of the plants on the living wall. It wasn't just smelling. It was high-speed chemical analysis. My mind dissecting the air itself. Identifying its components. Its history. Xylos, with its "significant bio-resonant cascades," suggested a complex, potentially hazardous atmosphere. Identifying trace contaminants *instantly* wasn't a luxury. It was survival.

"Finally, opto-neural calibration," Anya explained. Complex light patterns flickered inside the headset, synching with the bio-filaments at my temples, focusing my visual processing. "Optimizes visual cortex for broader spectrum input, enhances processing speed and filtering capabilities. Scarabite-7 emits a unique phase-energy signature, often masked by environmental interference." The briefing had emphasized these "unusual phase-resonant properties." "These phase-resonant properties are precisely what make it vital – capable of stabilizing the volatile energies needed to create and maintain Phase-Channel conduits, bypassing the limitations of standard hyperlane travel. This will allow you to perceive that signature directly, cutting through the interference, identifying the target." The light patterns intensified, swirling and shifting inside the headset, synching with the pulses beneath my skin. Then faded. Leaving a lingering warmth behind my eyes. A sense of heightened awareness settling in. Focusing, the ambient light in the room seemed richer, the edges of objects sharper, more defined. I could almost perceive faint electromagnetic fields humming around the active consoles. The energy flowing through them. A strange, exhilarating sensation. The world becoming layers of perceivable data. Optimizes visual cortex for broader spectrum input... Scarabite-7 emits a unique phase-energy signature, often masked. Perceive that signature directly... The words echoed in my mind. The focus on Scarabite-7 brought a flicker of memory. A connection to fragmented knowledge. It brought to mind fragmented records from early exploration attempts in this system, mentioning indigenous legends that spoke of 'weaving light' and 'singing crystals' – dismissed as primitive superstition by the initial survey teams. Resonating oddly with the energy patterns I was being trained to perceive. Was there truth in the old stories? Legends also spoke of 'unraveling light' and 'currents that bite' – warnings dismissed as primitive superstition. But now, facing the reality of Xylos and the need to perceive its volatile energies, the phrases felt chillingly specific. Echoing a deeper, ancient fear. Was there truth in the old stories? Was there truth in the warnings of a Great Mistake, of currents best left undisturbed? This calibration wasn't just about seeing better; it was about seeing the *specific* energetic signature of Scarabite-7 through Xylos's unique environmental "irregularities," as Sharma put it. It was the key to locating the resource without triggering unforeseen, potentially catastrophic reactions.

The entire process took under thirty minutes. A precise, technological ritual. The filaments were temporary, Anya assured me, dissolving harmlessly into my system after the mission. But the stimulated neural pathways, the heightened connections, would remain. A permanent alteration to my perception.

"The foundations for this," Anya remarked, observing the readouts on her pad. A small smile playing on her lips. A hint of shared understanding in her eyes. "Originated centuries ago. Early Watcher logs documented anomalous environmental perception – sensitivities we recently mapped to neural architectures, learned to replicate and amplify. Our ancestors navigated by feeling currents, by sensing the subtle energies of the world and the void. You navigate processing the raw data streams those currents represent, amplified and filtered." This tech didn't create the ability. It focused and amplified what was already there. Honed over generations of Watchers. A legacy I now carried into the unknown. A legacy now specifically honed for Xylos.

I sat up. The world intensely immediate. Almost painfully sharp. A flood of sensory information threatened to overwhelm. The station's operational symphony now has a thousand distinct notes. But my inherent acuity, amplified by the calibration, resolved it into usable data layers. The station's hum was now a complex symphony of operational frequencies, power flows, and subtle structural vibrations. The air told stories of its filtration process, the proximity of other personnel, the faint, lingering scent of Anya's own energy signature. Light carried information I'd never consciously perceived before, revealing hidden fields and subtle energy exchanges. It wasn't inherited magic, I reminded myself. It was targeted enhancement. Grounded in observation and analysis. Designed specifically for Xylos's hazardous, data-rich environment.

A tool. Finely calibrated. Ready for the task. I felt the weight of the mission settle upon me. The complexity of the unknown world awaiting my perception. But now, I also felt uniquely equipped to perceive its secrets. Not through ritual. Through senses pushed to the cutting edge of science and heritage. Pushed to handle the specific tremors, the specific contaminants, the specific energy signatures of Xylos.

The emerald world awaited. My perception was tuned. My journey, defined not just by ancestors and their ancient wisdom, but by where my skills could take me, by the mysteries I could unravel, was truly beginning. It began here, in this quiet room, preparing specifically for the unknown pulse and vibrant chaos of Xylos.

Chapter 3: Immersion in the Emerald Wild

Keket

After three months of travel, the Celestial Barque settled heavily onto alien soil. Landing struts groaned in Xylos's dense, humid air. The bridge, usually a space of familiar, layered darkness for standard vision, became an overwhelming symphony of information for me. A chaotic flood of sensory input. It threatened to drown my carefully calibrated senses. Consoles pulsed with faint heat signatures. They barely registered to normal sensors. But they were vivid to my enhanced perception. Like subtle energy flows tracing intricate patterns across the surfaces. Recycled air swirled in visible currents, revealed by minute temperature gradients that painted ghostly patterns in the air around me. Even dust motes suspended in the atmosphere emitted a faint bio-luminescent shimmer, likely from trace fungal spores, turning the air itself into a canvas of unexpected, living light. The Sensory Integration Suite enhancement, interwoven with my natural acuity, had granted me vision beyond the ordinary. Pushing my senses to their limit. But the sheer volume of input from this wildly alive world threatened to overload my systems. Buzzing behind my eyes like a swarm of angry data-bees. A constant, high-frequency static.

My hand ran along the cool console edge. Subtle vibrations provide tactile feedback. Layering another stream of data into my awareness. The bio-filaments beneath my skin, those intricate pathways now glowing with a soft, internal light – advanced bio-conductive polymers, not lapis lazuli, however much they echoed Nana's stories of ancient power – picked up unique frequencies resonating through the hull plating. Mapping stress from atmospheric entry and the impact of landing. These pathways transmitted data directly to my awareness. A constant, silent report on the Barque's physical state. A grounding presence amidst the alien sensory storm. Assuming the role of Captain and Chief Engineer – the duality felt right, reflecting the blend of spatial awareness and technical expertise needed for deep-space navigation . And, now, navigating this unpredictable surface – the weight of that role, the responsibility for my crew waiting below, settled heavily on my shoulders, anchoring me amidst the sensory chaos and driving my decisions.

My fingers manipulated the holographic interface before me with practiced speed. Data displays sharp and layered. Glyphs weren't just ancient symbols here; they were engineering schematics rendered in a common Sah Collective practice, mnemonic devices linking concepts to complex systems with names like Ankh (power stability, glowing green) and Djed (structural integrity, an unwavering line). It streamlined information, turning complex data into intuitively understandable patterns. A language my mind could process even as my senses reeled. Diagnostics scrolled across the interface as I ran through post-landing checks: Life support nominal, atmosphere processors optimal and cycling for high humidity, star drive standby humming faintly. The Barque, our vessel, felt stable beneath my feet. A familiar anchor in this alien storm of sensation.

"System status report, Ma'at," I stated, my voice cutting through the ambient hum of the ship and the perceived symphony of the world outside. The AI responded, its calm synthesized tone echoing optimized data processing. A familiar and reassuring presence. Not cosmic order, yet... sometimes, in the complex equilibrium it maintained, the way it processed vast amounts of data to keep us alive and functional, I sensed something akin to a digital Ka. A life-force woven from pure data, striving for balance. A foolish thought, perhaps, born of Nana's ancestral whispers and too little sleep. But Ma'at's unwavering efficiency and calm voice were a familiar anchor in the face of this overwhelming alienness. Sometimes, I swore I detected a hint of dry wit in its responses. A subtle personality that both comforted and unnerved me.

"Exterior atmospheric parameters?" I asked, my gaze flicking to the environmental readouts populating the interface. My mind is already trying to classify incoming data. The humidity was palpable even through the ship's environmental controls. A thick, heavy presence that made the air feel syrupy.

"Within life-support thresholds, Captain," Ma'at replied instantly, its data analysis complete. "Humidity 92%, consistent. Recommend sealed protocols for initial surveys, pending Wadjet probe sampling."

"Acknowledged. Long-range scans?" I prompted, bringing up the topographical and biological survey feeds, eager for more data, for something to analyze and understand.

"No concentrated Scarabite-7 signatures within ten kilometers," Ma'at confirmed, the scan results rendering as a swirling cloud of data points on the display. "Abundant, complex flora networks identified; significant bio-luminescence, active energy exchange. Smaller, chitinous organisms present, resembling terrestrial arthropods. Several larger lifeforms detected in surrounding forest; no overt hostility via spectral analysis. Behavioral patterns unknown." Unknown meant risk. Or opportunity. Depending on how you approached it.

I turned to the primary viewport – a vast expanse of hyper-dense crystal shielding, providing unparalleled clarity. Turning the alien world into a breathtaking, intimidating panorama. Xylos assaulted my senses. A riot of color and energy. It wasn't just a green riot. It was an explosion of life that vibrated through the ship's hull and into my very bones. Emerald, jade, malachite – the colors pulsed under the binary suns filtering through the dense canopy. Shifting and deepening with an intensity that made my head spin. Forcing me to adjust the viewport's filters slightly. Trying to reduce the overwhelming visual input to something manageable. The humidity clung to my skin, thick and heavy, even within the bridge's microclimate. Carrying the intoxicating, complex scents of alien pollen, decaying vegetation, and something else. Something wild and electric that made my heightened senses hum. Towering bioluminescent trees, massive trunks draped with pulsating mosses and dripping vines, formed a dense canopy that blotted out the sky. Their internal light adds another layer to the visual overload. Fungi glowed blue, green, violet on the forest floor, creating an ethereal underlight that made the ground seem to breathe with its own strange life. It was beautiful, yes, undeniably so. But also deeply unsettling. A world that felt ancient and terrifyingly alive. Utterly indifferent to our presence.

This was beyond anything my simulation training had prepared me for. This was the raw, unfiltered data I'd craved. The antidote to the hub's sterile efficiency. Antidote to endless lines of clean code. But craving it from afar was different from being immersed in its chaotic symphony. It felt less like stepping onto a new world and more like the world was stepping directly, forcefully, into my mind. My calibrated senses, honed to perceive the void's subtle energies, felt... assaulted. Like trying to drink from a firehose. Control, Keket, I ordered myself. Process. Analyze. Years of training kicked in, forcing the overwhelming input into manageable layers. But for a dizzying second, I felt utterly lost.

The weight of my crew's safety is sudden, crushing pressure against the sheer, unpredictable power of this alien place.

It was a far cry from the sterile efficiency of the orbital stations, the "ground static" I was so desperate to escape, but its intensity was a different kind of challenge.

As I continued to process the incoming data, my enhanced senses registered more than just the visual and olfactory overload. A low-frequency hum, almost below the threshold of hearing but felt deep in my bones, resonated from the planet's core – a pulse that seemed steady, yet carried a subtle, ancient tremor. Like the echo of a scream long past. It was a discordant note in the planet's otherwise vibrant energy field. A scar from a past wound that my Watcher senses instinctively picked up. Analyzing the planet's core energy readings streamed across the console, displaying immense power. But my enhanced senses registered more – a strange, rhythmic modulation beneath the raw data. A pulse that felt less like a geological process and more like a conscious beat, resonating on frequencies my Watcher senses instinctively recognized as 'aligned.' This world felt... aware. In a way I couldn't quantify with standard scientific terms.

Reviewing the long-range scans myself, focusing on the areas near the projected Scarabite-7 deposits, I noted anomalies that weren't just energy spikes. Certain geological formations showed signs of catastrophic, non-natural disruption – crystalline structures twisted and fused as if by immense, uncontrolled energy. Scars on the landscape that hinted at a violent past. Perhaps linked to the ancient tremor I felt. Adding to the unease, Bastet's voice crackled over internal comms, tight with professional concern. "Captain," she reported, "My environmental sensors are glitching near the projected settlement perimeter. Picking up transient energy signatures... they resolve then just vanish. Nothing in our database matches." A cold knot tightened in my stomach. Fleeting. Unidentifiable. Just like the glimpses in my calibration.

Activating internal comms, I addressed my crew. Their status icons glowing green on a separate display – Sekem, co-pilot, looked exhausted but alert, his face serene, focused on his own console; Bastet, engineering lead, reported from the ship's depths, her voice crisp and efficient despite the likely chaos of monitoring unfamiliar energy signatures; Joric, head of security, was a solid green icon, his status nominal. My team. Sekem's calm focus was a reassuring presence, a steady counterpoint to my own heightened state. Bastet's crisp reports grounded me in the familiar language of ship systems and operational parameters, even as she voiced her own professional concerns.

"Captain," Bastet's voice came through the comm, tight with professional unease. "My sensors are reading energy fluctuations down here that defy known physics. The power conduits are handling it, but this place feels... wrong, structurally. Like the architecture is alive, but temperamental." Her ingrained engineering skepticism was a stark contrast to the planet's wild energy, highlighting the gulf between our understanding and this reality.

"Acknowledged, Bastet," I replied, "Log everything. We're seeing similar anomalies up here."

"Captain," Sekem added, his voice calm but with an underlying tension. "The environmentals is... intense. My systems are flagging multiple unclassified biological and energy signatures. We're ready for deployment, but... vigilance is paramount."

"Understood, Sekem. Joric, status?"

"All internal security systems green, Captain. External scans show no immediate threats to the Barque, but the sheer volume of unclassified lifeforms is... significant. My team is on high alert." Joric's focus, as always, was on security, on the tangible threats. Their professionalism calmed the unease that always nipped at the edges of first contact, a reminder that I wasn't facing this alone, even if my perception of the world was currently far more complex than theirs.

"Acknowledged, all," I replied. "Standard exploration teams, all bio-scanners active, stay within comm range and line of sight where possible. We're here for Scarabite-7, but safety is paramount. Let nothing surprise us out there. Maintain open comms and report any anomalies immediately." My bio-filaments pulsed steadily beneath my skin. A low thrum that felt like an internal compass. Pointing towards unknown potential. A tool sharpened and ready.

Time to analyze, adapt, extract – the core mission, brought into sharp focus by the overwhelming, mysterious world outside. "Ma'at," I commanded, my gaze fixed on the emerald chaos of the viewport, the challenging beauty and unsettling anomalies of it demanding my full attention. "Deploy Wadjet probes. Begin atmospheric analysis, high-resolution ground scans, geological and bio-energy profiling. Flag all anomalous resonance patterns. Prioritize analysis of energy signatures near the Scarabite-7 deposits and any localized energy modulations that don't match the planet's core pulse."

Small, mirror-like spheres, each the size of a cold ball, detached from the Barque's hull with a faint click and levitated into the alien atmosphere. Sensors covered their mirrored surfaces, reflecting the lush environment as they hovered silently, analyzing and transmitting streams of data back to the ship. The Wadjet probe data streamed in, overwhelming in its detail. Amidst the expected readings for atmospheric composition and biological markers, my enhanced senses picked up faint, complex patterns of light and energy that didn't match known flora or geological activity – almost like a silent, intricate language being broadcast on frequencies my standard equipment couldn't register. What were these? Analyzing the limited long-range bio-signatures myself, I noted anomalies that didn't fit standard carbon-based life classifications – energy fields that shifted and modulated in complex ways, suggesting biological structures capable of interacting directly with ambient energy. What life was there? Analyzing the local energy field around the projected location of the Kryll settlement perimeter, I noted subtle, irregular modulations that didn't seem part of the main shield harmonics – almost like smaller, independent energy signatures operating just beneath the surface of the primary defense, hinting at internal divisions or factions. Observing the Kryll from a distance on the probe feeds, if possible, I noted subtle variations in their bioluminescent patterns or the style of their personal energy fields – not uniform, suggesting distinct groups or affiliations within the population, confirming the subtle energy anomalies I'd perceived.

"Let's see what this garden holds," I murmured, more to myself than the AI. My mind is already racing with the implications of the data. My enhanced vision, augmented tech, our training – these were our first tools in navigating this unknown. This mission, born from corporate need and Collective desperation, wasn't about reclaiming some mystical past, despite the echoes of my heritage. It was about securing the future, one measurement, one analysis, one step at a time, into the vibrant, unpredictable, and increasingly mysterious heart of Xylos.

Chapter 4: Resonant Frequencies and Invasive Light

Zephyr

Xylos wasn't merely the ground beneath my feet or the humid, life-rich air I breathed. It was the resonant pulse within my own bio-electric field. A symphony of memory and living energy. Connecting me intrinsically to every root, leaf, and crystal spire of this world. Here, adrift within that complex tapestry, tracing the life-pulses of colossal flora and the whispering mycorrhizal networks beneath the soil, I felt the potent coalescence of energy near Whispering Falls – the planet's sacred heart. The wellspring of our power. Movement was an effortless instinct. My faint energy signature modulates. Skin shifting hues in subconscious dialogue with the phosphorescent undergrowth. Seamless part of the planetary rhythm. It wasn't solitude. It was immersion. A deep, grounding sense of belonging. Of being a vital node in a vast, interconnected consciousness. Here, utterly connected, I was a single, harmonious element in Xylos's vast, breathing consciousness.

Then, disruption shattered the peace. A dissonance so profound it felt like a physical blow. A tearing in the fabric of the world's song. It wasn't sound, not initially. It was a jarring wrongness. A seismic tremor vibrating deep within the planet's core. Utterly alien. A vibration that felt wrong. Unnatural. Followed immediately by a wave of unfamiliar electromagnetic radiation. It scoured my senses like focused static. Like a harsh, alien light being shone into the deepest parts of my being. It ripped through the gentle fields I perceived, momentarily blinding me. Leaving phantom noise against my awareness. A screech of interference against Xylos's harmony. Violation, the thought screamed. Raw and instinctive. A deep thrum of distress echoing from the planet itself. Amplified through my own connection. Intrusion.

High above, a dense absence occluded the canopy's soft emerald glow – the intruder. Stark. Artificial. A jagged tear in the sky. Disrupting the local energy equilibrium. Its presence felt fundamentally incorrect. An oppressive, inorganic weight pressing down. Not just physically. Spiritually. Leaching the vibrancy from the air. Muting the planet's song. Deep unease tightened its grip. A cold dread coiling in my gut. A feeling that resonated with ancient,

19

buried fears. Caution, born from generations of isolation and the remembered trauma of the Great Mistake, warred intensely with the innate Kryll drive to understand anomalies. To map the unknown. To integrate new knowledge. Danger, a primal part of me whispered, urging retreat into the deep green embrace of the familiar forest. Disappear into the safety of Xylos's embrace. But what is it? another part countered, propelled by an essential, almost painful curiosity. The ancient Kryll thirst for understanding. That had led to so much good and terrible.

The desire to know won. Caution channeling itself into heightened stealth. Into the focused application of my abilities. I flowed through the undergrowth towards the source. A silent current through ferns pulsating with their own soft light. Utilizing the terrain. Modulating my light-bending chromatophores. Striving to become just another shadow. Indistinguishable from the dappled undergrowth. A part of the forest's natural camouflage. As I moved, I registered other shifts in the planetary hum – subtle disruptions in the mycorrhizal networks nearby, a faint, almost imperceptible increase in localized energy fields. Not the pure resonance of the Falls, but... organized. Structured. Signs that other Kryll, perhaps patrols or those with deeper connections to this sector, were also sensing the intrusion. Moving. Watching. The forest wasn't just hiding me; it was alive with unseen activity.

The alien vessel descended. A jagged wound of dull metal against the living emerald sky. Utterly devoid of the light and life that permeated my world. Settling with a sickening, grinding thud that reverberated through the very rock of the Falls. A physical echo of the spiritual violation. Its proximity was an agony. The way its presence felt – a cold, dead weight pressing down on Xylos, suffocating the vibrant energy that flowed through the land, muting the Heartstone's song – was a desecration. The Falls themselves seemed to weep. The crystalline water cascading with a sluggish, unnatural flow. The potent energy surrounding them muted. Struggling. As if the presence of the ship was draining the very life force from the land. It felt as if the vessel was sucking the life, the very Ka, from Xylos, and the planet's muted anguish echoed painfully within my own heart. A deep, sympathetic ache.

Unfamiliar chemical signatures tainted the humid air around the ship – sharp, sterile, metallic. Utterly alien against the rich, living scents of moss and damp earth, of blooming flora and flowing water. It smells... dead. Processed. Artificial. Wrong.

Suddenly, a focused energy beam lanced out from the vessel. Sweeping across the vegetation like a predator's gaze. Cold and clinical. Not light as I perceived it, not the soft, living glow of Xylos. But a concentrated EM pulse. Its frequency is unlike anything natural. Harsh. Structured. Incredibly invasive. A violation of the natural energy fields. As the beam grazed my hiding place beneath a pulsating frond, a cascade reaction, violent and uncontrollable, tore through my physiology. A painful resonance that overloaded my systems. No!

Pure panic surged. Overwhelming millennia of disciplined control. Overwhelming the training that kept my abilities in check. My chromatophores flared uncontrollably – not the subtle camouflage shifts or complex communication patterns of my people. A blinding, panicked, full-spectrum burst of light and color rippled across my skin. A raw, uncontrolled scream of energy. Physiological overload. A seizure of pigment and energy triggered by the alien frequency, by the invasive touch. Shock, searing disorientation, and the terrifying, naked feeling of exposure flooded me. Seen! Vulnerable! This involuntary betrayal by my own body felt catastrophic. A failure of control at the most critical moment. If the intruders saw... if my own kind, patrolling the perimeter energy fields, sensed this uncontrolled flare near an unknown arrival... suspicion would fall. Was I compromised? A conduit for this invasive energy? The fear was suffocating. A cold hand tightening around my chest.

Almost simultaneously, amidst the internal chaos, my electroreceptors registered an intricate energy pattern embedded within the invasive beam – complex, structured modulations, repeating in ordered sequence. A deliberate signal. Fractions of a second later, the exact same pattern echoed, sharp and chillingly precise, from the vessel's opening hatch. A specific energy signature, linking the scanning beam to whatever – whoever – emerged. What is this? A targeted signal? An attack frequency? A key? How does it... connect?

The vessel's hatch dilated, spilling forth a harsh, artificial light. It felt like shards of ice against my heightened senses. A violation. A desecration of Xylos's living glow. A figure appeared, encased in shielding material that muted its biological signature, moving with stiff, cautious deliberation. Utterly alien in its form and movement. Its form was jarringly alien – bipedal, starkly symmetrical, head encased in a smooth, opaque shell, external sensors panning methodically, clinically, assessing the environment with cold efficiency. I froze, suppressing my own energy signature frantically, forcing my riotous colors back under control, striving for absolute stillness. Observing from the deepest shadows beneath a tangle of ancient roots. Stillness. Blend. Become the forest. Disappear.

The figure left the hatch. Through transparent sections of its suit, or perhaps integrated directly into exposed skin – the distance and my own lingering disorientation made it hard to tell – I detected the source of the secondary energy signature: intricate, glowing blue pathways beneath the creature's skin, or woven into its strange coverings. It pulsed with the exact energy frequency and complex pattern embedded in the scanning beam. Artificial, I concluded instantly. Technological. A cold wave washed through me. Not the natural bioluminescence of our constellations, not the shared language of light and energy native to Xylos. This was evidence of unknown, invasive technology interacting with the environment and – horrifyingly, seemingly – directly with my own Kryll biology. Was the flare... intentional? Did it trigger me for a reason? Was this technology a weapon, or merely a tool?

But then my focus sharpened. Analytical assessment warring with something more fundamental. On the being itself. It was... intriguing. Quite short compared to the Kryll, but its form held a delicate, unexpected strength. A contained power. Its skin, where visible beyond the suit's collar, was a deep, rich umber, smooth and flawless like polished obsidian found deep within Xylos's caves. Etched upon its forearm, confirming my earlier perception, were those glowing blue lines, intricate and shifting, almost like living constellations mimicking the patterns I carried within my own lineage, yet fundamentally artificial. A blend of technology and biology I didn't understand. My people told fragmented stories of the Terrans of old Earth, before the Scattering, before the Great Mistake, and this being... it resembled those ancient, half-mythical descriptions.

Its head, freed now from the helmet which retracted seamlessly, was framed by a mass of dark, tightly coiled curls. A stark, living contrast to the pale, artificial light spilling from the ship. But it was the eyes that truly captivated me. Pulling my attention like nascent stars in the twilight sky. They were large and vividly green, luminous even in the dim undergrowth light. Holding a spark of fierce, undeniable intelligence. A depth of thought that drew me in. They lacked the multifaceted depth and layered perception of Kryll eyes. Possessing instead an unnerving, focused directness. It moved with a fluid grace, scanning its surroundings, though it lacked the powerful, overt musculature common among Kryll females. It was... striking. Beautiful. In a way that was utterly alien. Deeply unsettling. Yet undeniably compelling.

The figure – the Terran female – paused, her head tilting inquisitively. Her expression is guarded, analytical. Profoundly unreadable across the species divide. A mask of cautious assessment. Her optical sensors – those intense green eyes – swept the area again, pausing, lingering, passing directly over my shadowed hiding place. A spike of pure adrenaline, cold and sharp, coursed through me. Does it see me? Did my earlier flare betray my exact position? Had my attempt at suppression failed? The moment stretched, breathless and excruciatingly tense. The alien's attention seemingly fixed on the precise cluster of shadows where I pressed myself against the damp, mossy earth. Every fiber of my being screaming for stillness. I perceived minute shifts in her posture – analysis? Surprise? Threat assessment protocols surged. Every fiber of my being screaming DANGER! A handheld device, likely a scanner or weapon, lifted slightly in her hand. Ready.

Just as I prepared to melt deeper into the forest, accepting the necessity of retreat, of abandoning my observation for safety, the ground beneath her trembled again. A more significant aftershock from the vessel's landing, resonating through the Falls' delicate crystalline structures. A reminder of the disruption her ship represented. High above, a shelf of rock, heavy with dripping moss and crystalline growths, fractured with a sharp crack. Dust and pebbles rained down, followed by a larger, jagged chunk of crystal tearing loose, plummeting directly towards where the Terran stood frozen, momentarily distracted by the tremor. Her analytical mind is perhaps still processing the seismic data.

My warning cry was pure instinct – a sharp, trilling whistle ripped from my throat. Meaningless to her ears. But broadcasting pure alarm. A sound that resonated through the forest. Simultaneously, violating every protocol, every shred of ingrained caution, overriding the fear born of the Great Mistake and the dangers of interacting with outsiders, I surged forward from the shadows. Moving faster than I thought. Propelled by an instinct I didn't understand. I didn't try to shield her fully – too much risk of revealing myself, of exposing the depth of my connection to this place – but launched myself low, tackling her around the legs with bruising force, sending us both sprawling onto the mossy ground an instant before the heavy crystal chunk slammed into the earth where she had stood, shattering with explosive force. A sound that echoed the fracturing of my own carefully maintained control.

We landed in a tangle of limbs. The air is thick with crystal dust and the sharp scent of ozone. Her surprised cry was muffled against my shoulder pauldron. For a disorienting second, I was aware only of the startling warmth of her body against mine through the thin layers of her suit and my minimal armor. The surprisingly solid feel of her. The wild hammering of her heart against my ribs echoing my own frantic beat. The contact was electric. Unexpected intimacy forged in shared violence. A collision of worlds.

Then training reasserted itself. The ingrained discipline snapping back into place. I rolled clear, putting distance between us, even as I scanned the canopy for further threats. Adrenaline singing through my veins. She pushed herself, coughing from the dust. Those wide green eyes fixed on me now with shock, alarm, and dawning, furious comprehension. She had seen me. Truly see me. The warrior who had materialized from the shadows, tackled her, and now crouched defensively meters away. A being that defied her understanding. Retreat. Now. Don't panic. Calculated swiftness. Before her shock turned to action. Before her weapon came fully to bear. Before the moment passed. Before she could react further, before her weapon came fully to bear, I pushed off the ground and melted back into the dense foliage, weaving between the glowing trunks. Becoming one with the forest's familiar energy field. Like water rejoining a stream. Disappearing as quickly as I had appeared. Safe. Heart pounding. Hidden once more in the shadows. I processed the encounter. Violation. Fear. Invasive technology. The near-fatal rockfall. The shocking, involuntary contact. The fierce intelligence in those green eyes. The chilling certainty that this Terran female, Keket, and the invasive energy she carried, had irrevocably disturbed Xylos's ancient balance. It had triggered something within me, I didn't understand. And the undeniable, terrifying resonance I felt. Not just with the Path. But with her. A primal alarm, echoing a terror older than his own memories, screamed through his being – the chilling signature of off-world intrusion, a sound my ancestors had last heard during the unraveling.

Chapter 5: Warrior in the Emerald Wilds

Keket

My breath hitched, catching painfully in my throat like a trapped bird. The air, thick with the scent of damp earth, ozone, and alien pollen after the rockfall, seemed to solidify around me, pressing in. Through a shimmering curtain of phosphorescent vines just meters away, where moments before there had been only shadow and the echo of shattering crystal, my eyes locked onto him. Zephyr. The Kryll who had materialized from the vibrant chaos, tackled me to the ground with bruising force, saved me from a lethal chunk of falling rock, and vanished just as quickly back into the impossible green of this world. For a disorienting heartbeat, the universe paused. The overwhelming symphony of Xylos fading to a dull hum beneath the roaring in my ears. Replaced by the frantic beat of my own heart. The sharp sting of adrenaline.

I pushed myself up from the mossy ground, my limbs feeling heavy and uncoordinated, fighting the lingering disorientation. My hand, still slightly shaky, instinctively went to the pulse pistol holstered at my hip. A familiar weight against my thigh. A small, cold anchor in the surging tide of the unknown. Control, Keket. I ordered myself. My internal voice is sharp. A desperate overlay onto the lingering shock. Regain composure. Assess the situation. Analyze the threat. Maintain tactical awareness.

He was... a force of nature made flesh. Impossibly alien, yes. Utterly unlike any species cataloged by the Collective. Yet radiating a raw power and presence that defied easy categorization. Demanding immediate, undivided attention. Pointed ears, distinctly elfin yet fitting the sharp angles of his face, peeked through stark white hair. Long and curling slightly at the ends. Flowing like spun moonlight in sharp contrast to his deep, almost obsidian skin. He stood near giant, glowing cyan orchids whose alien beauty, moments ago breathtaking, was utterly eclipsed by his presence. He was a figure of stark, unexpected symmetry and power against the emerald glow of the phosphorescent undergrowth. Drawing the light to him. Seeming almost to absorb it. Training screamed. A thin, fraying lifeline in the face of being utterly, unexpectedly undone by sheer visual impact. Every protocol, every drill session on maintaining professional distance during unexpected contact, felt flimsy in

25

the face of this impossible being. He was an anomaly defying categorization. And my carefully constructed composure threatened to splinter just by looking at him.

He possessed a lean, well-defined, and undeniably powerful physique, emphasized by minimal dark-colored armor – sturdy bracers etched with unfamiliar geometric patterns covered his forearms, a complex chest harness of gleaming dark metal left much of his impressive torso bare but featured intricate gold detailing on the protective pauldrons, and several necklaces made of what looked like crystal shards or polished alien bone rested against his dark skin. Artifacts of a culture I knew nothing about. Hinting at tradition and strength. Intricate, glowing green tattoos, or perhaps bioluminescent pathways like my own tech but clearly organic, pulsed with faint light along his arms. Shifting and swirling like captured constellations against the dark canvas of his skin. Patterns hinting at a complexity, a connection to this world, I couldn't begin to decipher. But every cell in my body hummed with a different, deeper awareness – a resonance I couldn't name but felt echoing the strange energy signature I'd sensed earlier when his scanning beam hit. The one that seemed linked to my own bio-filaments. My amplified Watcher tech. It was an attraction, yes. More than attraction; it was a sudden, overwhelming wave of... recognition. Her bio-filaments, dormant pathways suddenly blazing with an answering light beneath her skin, sent a jolt through her system, making her gasp. The Watcher tech, designed to perceive cosmic energies, hummed with an intensity she'd never experienced, locking onto Zephyr's aura as if he were a newly discovered star, dangerous and undeniable, pulling her into an orbit she hadn't chosen but felt powerless to resist.

A primal, visceral pull that startled me with its intensity. Surprising in its suddenness. But tangled inextricably with fear and a profound, unsettling sense of the unknown. Is he the primary source of that energy signature? It pulsed from him, a palpable aura, a feeling that resonated with the faint tingling beneath the bio-filament patterns on my own skin, the light that had answered his beam. An echo of recognition, illogical yet insistent, resonated deep within me, a sense of inevitability clashing violently with my need for control, with the mission parameters.

His face, framed by the startling white hair, held high cheekbones and a strong, resolute jaw – arresting, intense, unsettlingly beautiful in its alien structure. But his eyes... They were luminous, glowing white orbs without discernible pupils, holding an intelligence that felt ancient, vast, and unnervingly direct. They fixed on me, not like human eyes scanning a surface for threats or information, but like multifaceted sensors piercing through layers, analyzing structure, energy, intent. It was as if I were the specimen under a microscope – pinned, dissected, laid utterly bare to his alien perception. A shiver, born of adrenaline and something more profound, a dizzying mix of primal fear and an unwelcome sense of exposure, ran down my spine. Don't stare, Captain. Heat flooded my cheeks. A humiliating betrayal of the cool professionalism I was desperately trying to project. Assess. Report. Get it together. I chided myself inwardly, forcing my gaze away for a millisecond, scanning the dense foliage around him for others, for threats I might have missed in my shock, for an escape route if needed, before it snapped back, a moth drawn helplessly to a mesmerizing, potentially lethal flame.

I forced my feet forward, damp leaves whispering like warnings under my standard-issue boots. One step. Another. Asserting control through simple, physical action, putting distance between the rockfall site and myself. My hand instinctively rose, brushing the familiar lines on my forearm where the filaments lay beneath the skin – a physical anchor, a reminder of the tech, the training, the mission. Professionalism. Protocol. First Contact. My heart hammered like a trapped bird against my ribs, threatening to crack my composure with every frantic beat.

"Greetings," I managed, the standard Terran syllable loud, horribly intrusive in the breathing stillness of the alien forest. Feeling clumsy and inadequate even as I spoke it. He won't understand, my logical mind supplied instantly, running through known linguistic databases. Universal translators require baseline data; the Barque has nothing on Kryll linguistics. This is probably useless, but it's protocol. But the Captain followed protocol. Establish peaceful intent. Project confidence even when knees felt weak and adrenaline made my limbs feel heavy.

"I am Captain Keket of the Celestial Barque. Sah Collective Registry. We mean no harm. We come in peace." I held my breath, watching his face for any sign of recognition. Any flicker of understanding.

He simply... watched. Those luminous white eyes seemed to see through the uniform, past the rank insignia, searching deeper, analyzing the energy patterns I emitted, perhaps even the frantic bio-signals of my racing heart, the subtle tremor in my hands I fought to conceal. His head tilted slightly, a slow, fluid movement, the white curls shifting like a moonlit waterfall around his dark face. Then came sounds – his sounds. Melodic clicks, soft, resonant whistles, complex tones layered in ways that defied human phonetics. Utterly alien, yet possessing a strange, compelling rhythm that resonated not purely in my ears, but somewhere deeper, felt along the energy pathways of my tech, a subtle vibration against my enhanced senses, almost like music I couldn't quite decipher. Nothing like it existed in the Barque's extensive linguistic database. Frustration pricked sharp and unwelcome, cutting through the lingering awe. How could we communicate? How could I negotiate for Scarabite-7, ensure my crew's safety, if we couldn't even establish basic understanding?

Undergrowth rustled nearby, drawing my gaze, snapping my attention away from the enigma before me. Two more figures emerged silently from the shadows, melting into view almost as suddenly as the first. Their movements are as graceful and silent as his. Similar athletic build, same obsidian skin, though their hair was dark and braided, and they lacked the glowing markings of the warrior before me. They moved towards him with undeniable deference. Their eyes – dark and piercing, lacking the unsettling luminescence of his – flicking between him and me. Filled with suspicion directed at me. But clear respect for him. Their energy signatures, visible to my enhanced senses, seemed... different. Not uniform. One pulsed with a sharp, almost aggressive energy. The other with a guarded, cautious hum. Subtle, but noticeable. Hinting at more than just a united front. Whispering of potential divisions.

One addressed him in the same clicking, melodic language, the tone vibrating with unmistakable... reverence. It clicked. Stars above, Keket, get it together. Not just a local hunter or scout encountered by chance, startled by our arrival. Their deference, his quiet, contained command, the sheer weight of his presence... This wasn't just an inhabitant. This was someone important. A leader. Definitely a leader. The thought resonated with startling clarity, cutting through the haze of my initial shock and focusing my strategic mind. He was observing us, assessing the threat we posed to his people, to this vibrant, sacred-feeling sanctuary, not just reacting to an intrusion. And I, Captain Keket, was standing here distracted by his arresting appearance and my own reeling senses when I should be formulating strategy, assessing defenses, calculating odds, preparing for a potentially hostile encounter with a sovereign power. Get it together. Your crew is waiting. This mission, my crew waiting anxiously in orbit, maybe even the stability of Collective supply lines – it all just became infinitely more complicated, resting on interaction with a being whose motivations were unknown and whose presence scrambled my tactical thinking, threatening to override my training with something far more visceral. This distraction itself felt like a vulnerability. A potential mission failure point originating within me. Not from an external threat.

Okay, plan B. Gestures. Necessary, however crude. A universally understood language, even basic. Slow, deliberate movements, hoping to convey meaning through action. I tapped my chest. "Keket. Captain." I pointed skyward, indicating the direction of orbit, then back towards the faint outline of the Barque's ramp, partially visible through the trees. My ship. My responsibility. "Ship. Celestial Barque. We come from... far away." I made a broad, sweeping gesture towards the canopy and the star-dusted void beyond. "Stars." I watched his face, searching for any flicker of comprehension. Any shift in his posture. Is any of this getting through?

The warrior – I couldn't think of him any other way now – continued his intense, silent observation. The mask of regal composure firmly in place. But was that...? Yes. A flicker deep within those luminous eyes. Not hostility, not aggression, not fear. Something closer to... intense, analytical curiosity. Hope surged, fragile but insistent, pushing back against the fear and frustration. Maybe that energy signature, that strange feeling of recognition pulsing between my tech and his biology... maybe it was a bridge. Something deeper than words. Something that transcended language barriers. I had to believe it. Because navigating this emerald wilderness, surviving this first contact, just became infinitely more complex – and potentially far more dangerous – dealing with someone holding such clear authority, someone whose gaze seemed to see right through my carefully constructed façade, someone who resonated with my very being in a way I couldn't explain. Deep breaths, Keket.

Recalibrate. The mission difficulty just cranked itself to maximum. And the most unpredictable, and perhaps most compelling, variable was standing right in front of me.

Chapter 6: A Symphony of Understanding

Keket

His luminous green eyes, startlingly vivid against his obsidian skin, held mine. Expectant. Searching. The silence stretched, thick and heavy with unspoken questions, broken only by the complex, multi-layered sounds of the Xylos jungle – the chirps, clicks, and unseen rustlings forming a disorienting backdrop to the tension coiling between us. Communication was paramount. Strategically vital. Yet my earlier attempts at crude gestures felt laughably inadequate now, especially facing someone radiating his palpable status and quiet intensity. Stars above, I needed a bridge, and fast. Right, the implant. Ma'at. No time to waste.

"Ma'at," I subvocalized. The mental command is a desperate lifeline back to the Celestial Barque's cool logic. Orbiting unseen above this overwhelmingly vibrant world. "Prioritize full linguistic download of recorded Kryll vocalizations from the initial encounter and passive environmental capture. Input directly to neural memory. Highest priority." It was a brute-force method, bypassing standard translation matrices for direct absorption – a risk, potentially disorienting, but necessary. The connection was seamless, my private channel to the ship's AI humming silently.

"Acknowledged, Captain Keket. Initiating neural download. Estimated duration: 4.7 seconds," Ma'at's calm synthesized voice echoed only within the architecture of my mind. Relief washed over me. Sharp and immediate. But it was instantly followed by a disorienting wave of tingling static blooming behind my eyes. Spreading through my skull. It wasn't just data; it felt like raw concepts, alien syntax structures, fragments of cultural context – glimpses of interconnectedness, reverence for crystalline structures, a deep bio-resonance with the planet itself – flooding my consciousness alongside vocabulary and grammar.

Initializing linguistic architecture... Kryll language file loading... Encoding complex phonetics... Warning: Significant data gaps detected. Certain conceptual frameworks appear deliberately obscured or absent from basic vocalizations. Attempting pattern recognition... Incomplete.

Necessary violation, but invaluable. My head swam. The air is heavy with humidity and alien pollens. The warrior's earlier melodic clicks and whistles, previously just noise, blurred into a chaotic symphony before slowly resolving, like a complex equation finding its solution, into distinct sounds. Layers of potential meaning clicking into place. The Ma'at's warning lingered, a subtle note of caution beneath the unfolding understanding. Deliberately obscured? Hidden knowledge? What secrets were woven into this language?

The world sharpened. The very air feels different. Charged now with the breathtaking potential for understanding. I took a deep, grounding breath, trying to steady myself against the lingering mental static and the unsettling hint of hidden depths. I looked back at the alien warrior. The being of dark skin, stark white hair, and startling eyes.

"Zephyr," I said, testing the name Ma'at had likely extrapolated from the deferential tones of the other Kryll. The alien syllables felt surprisingly natural on my tongue, less clumsy than I'd feared. A tentative bridge cast across the vast chasm separating our species. Did it work? Gods, let it work.

Surprise flickered distinctly across his sculpted features, widening those intense eyes fractionally before his guard snapped back into place. Then, astonishingly, a slow, guarded smile touched his lips, easing some of the rigid tension in his stance, and strangely, easing something tight in my own chest I hadn't realized I was holding. Relief, potent and dizzying, washed through me. Connection established. His reply flowed, the clicks and whistles now perceived as comprehended language, liquid and graceful, holding nuances of tone I could now interpret.

"I am Zephyr Kryll," he confirmed, his voice a resonant baritone, deeper now that I understood the cadence. "A protector of the Weaving Crystals." Protector. The title resonated powerfully with his watchful stance, his inherent authority, the way he seemed attuned to the very energy of this place. This was no mere tribal chief; his role was intrinsically tied to the planet's core systems, perhaps even to the Scarabite-7 itself. Serious indeed.

I offered a slight, formal bow, the Collective gesture for acknowledging sovereignty, hoping it translated across species as respect. "Keket," I responded, my name feeling blunt and utilitarian compared to the elegance of his Kryll speech. "Captain of the Celestial Barque. Traveler from the stars beyond your sky."

"You have come far, Keket of the stars," Zephyr replied, his voice regaining some of its formal quality, though the curiosity remained potent in his gaze. There was careful assessment in his tone now, a subtle probing beneath the surface politeness. "You seek something here. Something within our Weaving Crystals." It wasn't phrased as a question.

He knew. Or suspected strongly. My heart gave a hard jump against my ribs. How? Had the ship's initial scans been so transparent? Or was it his connection to this place, some way he could sense intent? Honesty, my gut screamed. Deception felt impossible, suicidal even, faced with that piercing intelligence. I met his gaze directly, squaring my shoulders, the Captain taking precedence over the reeling woman.

"We seek a specific mineral matrix," I stated, keeping my explanation simple, technical, and factual. "Exhibiting unique phase-resonant energy properties vital for stabilizing conduits between systems. We call it Scarabite-7." I laid out the core truth, omitting the desperation, the crumbling Collective infrastructure. "Our ability to journey between the stars depends on acquiring stable sources of it."

I braced myself for denial, accusation, perhaps even hostility – the reaction of any sovereign power to an outsider admitting they wanted to extract a vital resource. Instead, his expression showed no alarm, no immediate suspicion. It softened slightly, becoming thoughtful, introspective. His gaze dropped from my face to my forearm, specifically to the bio-filament patterns still glowing faintly beneath my skin. My tech? Then, his own skin... shifted. A subtle ripple ran across the visible muscle of his bicep, and intricate patterns, similar to the tattoos I'd noted earlier but more complex, bloomed and faded across his dark skin, shimmering with a soft internal green light that echoed the nearby foliage. It was mesmerizing, deeply unsettling, and beautiful. Not identical to my star charts, yet possessed of a similar cosmic, patterned complexity. What is he doing? Is that communication? Biology?

"The light," he murmured, his voice low, regaining that resonant hum that seemed to vibrate the humid air around us. "When your vessel arrived... I felt it. A specific energy signature, structured, artificial. Like a dissonant star igniting where none should be." He looked back at me, those green eyes searching again, penetrating, assessing my reaction. "And then, moments later, your light answered mine. On your arm." He tilted his head. "It was... a conversation."

The energy! That feeling I'd dismissed as proximity interference, the faint resonance between my tech and the environment... a conversation? Unintentional, but based on his reaction, undeniably real. "My... my bio-integrated systems," I stammered slightly, feeling strangely exposed, my hand unconsciously tracing the lines on my arm. "They are based on ancient Terran star charts passed down through my lineage – the 'Watchers'. They react to ambient energy fields, aid navigation... they are amplified by internal tech for deep space use... I didn't know they could..." Talk? Interact on this level? The idea was scientifically staggering, bordering on the mystical aspects of my heritage Nana whispered about.

Zephyr's own light pulsed again, a soft, rhythmic beat along his arms, seemingly involuntary. "But not just to me, Keket of the stars," he continued, his voice regaining intensity, his gaze sharpening. "When your vessel descended, the flora near the Falls... responded. Their natural luminescence shifted, pulsed in complex patterns never witnessed before. You... your arrival, your energy, your technology... it seems to have forged an unintended connection to Xylos's living heart." Plants? Reacting to the Barque's energy fields? My scientific mind reeled, grappling with the impossibility. Could my 'Watcher' sensitivity, amplified by tech, be doing more than just reading energy signatures? Was I somehow... broadcasting? Interacting with the planet's bio-field on a fundamental level I didn't understand?

Zephyr's gaze locked onto mine again, sharp, penetrating, filled now with an intensity that sent a fresh shiver down my spine. It was a strange, potent mix of scientific awe and profound, almost dangerous, curiosity.

"My city," he said, his voice dropping, becoming intimate, conspiratorial, pulling me closer psychologically despite the physical distance. "It lies hidden. Protected by an energy field woven from the Weaving Crystals beneath us – Scarabite-7, the source you seek." An invitation? Access? My strategic mind seized on the opening, even as astonishment warred with caution. Access granted?

But there was always a 'but'. His next words confirmed it, landing like a physical weight. "I would show it to you, Keket. Share its light, allow you to see the source." He paused, the weight of the condition falling heavily, ominously, between us in the suddenly charged air. "But only if you can explain this phenomenon. Only if you can tell me how you, traveler from the void, unknowingly spoke to my world's heart. How your light reached the plants... and resonated directly with me." Explain? How could I possibly explain something that defied my understanding of physics, biology, and technology?

The pressure mounted, sharp and immediate. My mission, my crew's safety, access to the vital Scarabite-7, all apparently hinged on unraveling a mystery embedded in my lineage, my biology, amplified by technology I barely understood myself, and explaining it to the satisfaction of this enigmatic, powerful alien leader. This felt less like a negotiation, more like being presented with an impossible riddle at the gates of a mythical city. Gods below. This just keeps getting more complicated. The path forward seemed simultaneously opened and completely blocked, a potential dead end paved with impossible expectations.

Chapter 7: Echoes in the Crystal Labyrinth

Keket

Walking beside him deeper into the crystal labyrinth felt utterly surreal. A descent into a world woven from light and ancient stone. Light, fractured and multiplied by countless crystalline surfaces, painted the towering walls in a living, shifting kaleidoscope of emerald, amethyst, and sapphire hues. The air hummed with a low, resonant frequency. Felt in the soles of my boots. Felt in the fillings in my teeth. A subtle vibration that seemed to align with the faint pulse of my bio-filaments. A deeper resonance than the station's sterile hum. Understanding Zephyr's melodic Kryll language, thanks to Ma'at's constant feed woven seamlessly into my thoughts, felt almost second nature now. As we passed through the plaza, my enhanced senses picked up on subtle energy signatures, a low hum of discontent I'd learned to recognize in the less harmonious sectors. I noticed a small group, their bioluminescence muted, their stances rigid. Faction Twelve, I noted mentally. Their discord was a constant undercurrent in the city's song.As we passed through the plaza, my enhanced senses picked up on subtle energy signatures, a low hum of discontent I'd learned to recognize in the less harmonious sectors. I noticed a small group, their bioluminescence muted, their stances rigid. Faction Twelve, I noted mentally. Their discord was a constant undercurrent in the city's song. A strange intimacy forged in shared syntax. Allowing me to appreciate the subtle cadence of his voice as he spoke of this hidden path. The rise and fall echoing the very pulse of the mountain around us.

"These caves..." I began, my voice sounding small. Absorbed by the echoing hush that swallowed sound. A stark contrast to the vibrant hum of the crystal. I gestured towards a massive, sharply faceted formation glistening with internal moisture. Its geometry is impossible by Terran standards. Defying conventional geology. "Are they part of the energy field protecting your city? Are they conduits for the shield?" My gaze drifted, taking in the impossible geometry, the sheer scale of the crystalline formations. Trying desperately to anchor myself in practicalities. In tactical assessment. In the quantifiable. Is this a structural component? An energy conduit? How is this stable?

Zephyr shook his head. The movement is fluid and precise. Drawing my attention back to him. Faint blue highlights woven into his long black braids caught the shifting light like trapped nebula fragments against his dark skin. A subtle beauty that was undeniably distracting. Light played across the strong planes of his face, highlighting high cheekbones, the smooth richness of his dark skin... I forced my eyes away, back to the crystal strata. Evidence of geologic time etched in stone. The slow, deliberate growth that spoke of immense power. And patience. Analyze the environment, Captain. Threat assessment. Resource potential. But my gaze kept snagging, lingering moments later, on the subtle ripple of muscle beneath his skin as he moved. The inherent grace that spoke of power held easily in check. It was a purely unprofessional, unwelcome, visceral appreciation for his alien appeal. A distraction I couldn't afford. Especially here. Gods. He moved like starlight made solid. Impossible. Utterly captivating. Every flex of muscle beneath his scaled skin, the fluid line of his stride – power contained. A guardian carved from the world itself. And my gaze kept snagging. Lingering.A distraction I couldn't afford. Especially here.

"No, Keket. The primary shield lies beyond," his voice held the deep, resonant knowledge of lived history. A tone that resonated with the very hum of the caves. With the planet's energy. "It is woven from the energy flowing through these crystals, amplified and focused by the Heartstone. This path... it is a secret way. Known only to the lineage of Protectors." His voice dropped, the melody flattening into something heavy with sorrow and caution. "Long ago, before the field could shield us completely from all threats, there was... vulnerability. An error in judgment. A Mistake made by those who came before me. A time of Unraveling."

He didn't look at me, his gaze fixed on a scarred crystal wall nearby. Where the growth seems stunted, twisted, as if recovering from ancient trauma. Not just stunted, but *violently* disrupted. Jagged fissures radiated from a central point, filled not with glowing moisture but a dull, obsidian-like charring. It felt like a physical manifestation of pain, of energy unleashed and uncontrolled, a raw wound on the planet itself mirroring a deeper trauma. A physical scar on the planet itself mirroring a deeper wound.

"It cost us dearly. My parents... they were lost to the chaos that erupted."

"The very air screamed that cycle, they say. The sky split, and the currents tore at the fabric of everything. Many believed Xylos wept, its energy unraveling alongside our own understanding."

He paused, the weight of the memory palpable. "Afterward, the knowledge of this path, and the deepest understanding of the Path itself, was sealed away. Not just from outsiders, but from certain factions within our own society who sought to misuse its power, to weaponize it rather than seek harmony. The fear of repeating that mistake, of unleashing that chaos again, runs deep." A shadow passed over those startling green eyes – not just recollection, but deep, resonant guilt. A burden he carried for generations past. Real, profound. I suddenly sensed the immense weight he carried. A failure from generations past anchoring him despite the imposing aura of command he projected. In that moment, he wasn't just the enigmatic alien leader. He was someone carrying history, loss, responsibility. A burden etched into his very being. Shaped by the choices of those who came before him. It made him feel... unexpectedly, dangerously real. A vulnerability that resonated with my own carefully buried fears of failure, of inadequacy, of the consequences of my own choices. The silence between us was heavy with the ghosts of the Great Mistake and the crushing weight of command.

"But you... you travel between the stars! You navigate the void I have only dreamed of!" His voice held a note of pure wonder. A longing that surprised me. "What wonders have you seen out there, Keket? What worlds exist beyond our sky? What drives your people to traverse such emptiness?" The transition was dizzying – the cautious protector burdened by history replaced in an instant by someone undeniably drawn to the vast unknown I represented. It was... endearing, in a way that disarmed my internal defenses, chipping away at the careful walls I'd built.

"Many," I replied, a small, involuntary smile tugging at my lips. It felt strange, almost illicit, sharing glimpses of the void here, in this hidden, ancient place. A sanctuary built on secrets and loss. I chose my words carefully, selecting images that conveyed the scale and diversity without revealing strategic vulnerabilities. Trying to translate the intangible feeling of space into something he could grasp. "Worlds of fire, orbiting too close to their parent stars, their surfaces molten glass. Worlds of ice, where oceans lie miles beneath frozen surfaces, teeming with life that never sees the light of a sun. Gas giants with storms larger than inhabited planets, nebulae stretching across light-years like painter's canvases of cosmic dust and light... Civilizations built on wildly different principles, some technological, some biological, some beyond easy definition, existing in harmony or conflict, driven by survival, expansion, curiosity."

I saw the fascination deepen in his eyes. His head tilted slightly as he absorbed my words. Processing concepts utterly alien to his rooted existence. He peppered me with questions – about propulsion systems, about alien biologies I'd encountered, about the structure and politics of the Collective, about the balance between technology and nature in other systems – his inherent cosmic curiosity momentarily overriding his ingrained caution. His role as Protector. He asked about the Sanction, about Diaspora, about how humanity maintained its identity across the stars. This blend of solemn responsibility and wide-eyed wonder... it was captivating, drawing me in despite my resolve to maintain professional distance. We discussed the concept of isolation versus connection, the price of security, the drive to explore versus the need to protect what you have. He listened intently to my explanations of corporate structures, the relentless pursuit of profit, the "ground static" that drove me away from that life, asking probing questions about the human cost of expansion.

We stopped beside a cluster of vibrant green crystals pulsing with a soft, rhythmic internal light. The air around them feels warmer. More charged. The energy is almost palpable. Zephyr reached out, his hand strong, long-fingered, elegant, gently brushing the smooth, cool surface. The lean muscles in his forearm flexed subtly – a purely physical observation that sent an unexpected jolt through me, a shiver down my spine. Stop noticing things like that, Keket. Focus. "Look," he murmured, his attention momentarily captivated by the crystal's glow, his voice soft with reverence. Then, with a swift, fluid motion, he plucked a single luminous bloom growing from a crevice, its petals radiating a soft, warm light. A delicate counterpoint to the massive crystals. A piece of the living cave. He turned, offering it to me. His gaze was direct. Holding a question I couldn't yet answer.

My breath caught in my throat. The gesture was so simple. So personal. So unexpected. Coming from this imposing, serious figure who carried the weight of his world's history. A playful glint sparked in his green eyes. A flash of unexpected charm that disarmed me completely. Bypassing my analytical mind. Melting away layers of my carefully constructed defenses. My heart performed a ridiculous little flip-flop against my ribs. This wasn't protocol. This wasn't diplomacy. This felt like... something else entirely. Something far more dangerous in its potential intimacy. My fingers closed automatically around the smooth, surprisingly warm stem. The bloom's light pulsing gently against my skin. A soft, living warmth that felt strangely comforting. The air between us thickened, not with humidity, but with unspoken awareness.

We stood in silence for a long moment, the only sounds the soft hum of the crystals, the gentle drip of water, and the frantic beat of my own pulse in my ears. I looked at the bloom in my hand, then up at him. He wasn't looking at the flower. His luminous eyes were fixed on me. Searching. Assessing. But with a new depth I hadn't seen before. I saw the weariness etched around his eyes, a reflection of the burden he carried, but also a flicker of longing, a quiet intensity that mirrored the restlessness within me. He saw my own carefully masked fatigue, the determination in my jaw, the flicker of awe in my eyes as I took in his world. In that shared silence, amidst the ancient grandeur, something shifted. It was the intimacy of being truly seen, truly understood, on a level that transcended words and cultural barriers. It was terrifying, and undeniably compelling.

Then his voice shifted again, dropping lower, regaining its seriousness, the commander reasserting himself, though the warmth lingered in his gaze. "Your connection to Xylos... it intrigues me profoundly, Keket. Our oldest legends speak of the planet itself interacting with energies from beyond the sky. Could your arrival... your unique resonance... be part of fulfilling those old stories? Could you be the counterpart spoken of?" His gaze was intense again, searching, analytical, probing the depths of my being. The charming alien was gone, replaced by the warrior and protector, always analyzing, trying to understand my place, my potential meaning in his world, in the ancient prophecies that shaped his people's destiny.

The narrow path opened abruptly, stunningly, into a vast cavern. Crystalline structures soared towards an unseen ceiling, vaulting arches and intricate lattices catching and refracting the ambient light like the skeletal ribs of some colossal, ancient beast fashioned from pure energy and stone. Waterfalls of light cascaded down walls embedded with enormous crystals, filling the space with a breathtaking, ethereal glow. The sheer, otherworldly beauty stole my breath, leaving me momentarily speechless. My scientific mind struggles to process the impossible scale and structure. The raw power contained within the living stone.

"It's... incredible, Zephyr," I whispered. The words are inadequate. Swallowed by the vastness. By the profound sense of being in a place of immense, ancient power. Against this breathtaking backdrop, he looked magnificent. Perfectly at home. Both guardian and enigma woven into the fabric of this impossible place.

"It is our heart," he replied, his voice quiet with fierce pride. His gaze sweeping the cavern with reverence before returning to me. His eyes held mine with an intensity that made breathing difficult again. The air charged with the weight of the place and his presence. With the unspoken potential that hung between us. "But you... you journey through the void. You spoke of needing Scarabite-7 for your people's survival. Is it truly worth traversing such emptiness, such danger, risking everything for survival?" The question landed heavily, forcing the sharp conflict within me to the surface. The core dilemma of my life. The constant pull between duty and desire. Between safety and the unknown. My duty to the Sah Collective, the faces of Sekem and Bastet and the others relying on me, the vital, non-negotiable importance of the mission – it all felt stark and somehow diminished against the overwhelming, ancient wonder of Xylos and the undeniable, magnetic pull I felt towards Zephyr himself. His nearness was a constant hum beneath my thoughts, disrupting my focus, challenging my priorities, making the sterile logic of the Collective feel distant and cold.

"It is vital," I managed. The words feel flat. Inadequate in this place of living light and impossible beauty. In the face of his profound connection to this world. "For our continued survival between the stars. For the future of our scattered people. It is our path."

Zephyr's gaze softened, and for a moment, I thought I saw a flicker of genuine understanding, perhaps even sympathy, in those luminous green depths, a recognition of the burden of leadership and survival. "Survival is a powerful motivator," he conceded, acknowledging the weight of my words, the shared imperative that drove our peoples. He paused, the silence amplifying the soft, resonant hum of the giant crystals around us, the heartbeat of his world, the energy that flowed through him. Then he added, his voice a low rumble that seemed to vibrate through the cavern floor. Intimate. Loaded. "As is... connection." He let the word hang there. Intimate. Loaded. His gaze fixed unwaveringly on mine. Bridging the distance between us with its weight. With the shared understanding that had grown between us in this hidden place. My heart hammered against my ribs. Connection. Not just scientific curiosity, not just resource acquisition. Not anymore, was it? We were too close, the air charged with something unspoken, something far more complex than first contact protocols, something that resonated on a level that defied my scientific understanding.

"Your own connection to Xylos," I said quickly, my voice a little breathless, deliberately steering the conversation back towards safer, more analytical ground, trying to reassert control over the situation and my own reactions. "It seems almost spiritual. My background is science, Zephyr, understanding the mechanics of the universe, of energy flows and material composition. I rely on data, on logic." I needed those logical walls back, solid and defensible, against the rising tide of something I couldn't quantify. Something that felt dangerously close to the mystical.

"And yet," Zephyr countered gently, a knowing, almost teasing smile touching his lips, seeing right through my deflection with unnerving ease, his eyes holding a depth of understanding that unnerved me. "You spoke to the plants, Keket of the stars. Your amplified energy, born of science and heritage, interacted with mine in ways that defy mere mechanics. You felt the resonance. You saw glimpses of my world, and I, yours." He held my gaze, challenging my scientific worldview, pushing me to consider possibilities beyond my current understanding. "Perhaps... there are more connections woven into the fabric of the universe than your science has yet charted. Maybe space isn't just mechanics. Perhaps it is also... harmony."

Warmth spread through me, entirely unrelated to the cave's ambient temperature, a response to his words, his gaze, the undeniable pull, the sense of shared discovery. He wasn't wrong. Logic felt thin and brittle here, in this place of living crystal and ancient power, standing beside this enigmatic warrior who seemed to embody the very essence of his world. As his gaze held mine, amidst the silent, crystalline grandeur, I felt that undeniable pull sharpen into something acutely personal. Recognition. The keen intelligence, the deep-seated curiosity residing within this alien warrior resonate strongly with my own core, even as his physical presence stirred something fundamentally different, something increasingly difficult, and perhaps foolish, to ignore. The mission was no longer just minerals. It was about him, this place, and the impossible, undeniable connection forged between us in light and shadow, in shared vulnerability and growing understanding. I had no idea where this path was leading, only that it felt both terrifying and inevitable.

Chapter 8: Harmonies Forged in Starlight

Zephyr

As the ship ascended later that cycle, a sleek silver scar shrinking against the twilight hues bathing the sky above the cave mouth, it left behind an unnerving quiet. Amplifying the dissonant thrum beneath my own skin – a resonance tuned solely, inexplicably, to her. Keket. Even the familiar, grounding vibration of Xylos flowing through the crystal around me felt different now, subtly altered by the echo of her presence. Relief, yes – the departure of her Terran crew simplified matters, removed potentially watchful, mistrustful eyes from the immediate vicinity of my hidden city. But it left her here. With me. Keket. A solitary star fallen into my hidden world, a variable of immeasurable potential and risk. Standing beside her amidst the familiar, grounding vibration of Xylos flowing through the crystal around us, I felt the staggering vastness she represented press in on me. More than the stars. More than the void she traversed. The pull was *her*. A fierce, bright core of defiance. A yearning that called to something ancient within me. I saw galaxies reflected in the depths of her dark green eyes, sensed the knowledge of suns I had only dreamed of chartered behind her steady, analytical gaze. A profound, aching longing resonated deep within my core – not just the childish wish to see those wonders, to traverse the void myself, but a desperate yearning to bridge the impossible distance between my rooted existence, my duty to this shielded world, and the boundless, untethered wandering she embodied. Could Xylos, could I, offer sanctuary, a counterpoint to the cold void she traversed? Could the deep, ancient harmony of my world resonate with the restless fire that drove her?

Intertwined with that longing, a fierce, protective urge arose, sharp and unexpected: the need to share the intricate beauty of my world, this sanctuary woven from light and crystal, from ancient energy and hard-won survival. To show her what we guarded, what we were. Perhaps here, grounded by Xylos's heart-song, by the tangible reality of a world deeply connected to its energy, she could find the meaning her restless energy seemed to chase among the stars, the purpose that eluded her in the sterile, corporate-driven void she described. The restlessness I had sensed when our minds brushed earlier – it felt like a reflection of the void itself, a lack of anchor, a spirit adrift. Could this place, could we, be that anchor?

The decision solidified, a crystalline structure forming rapidly within my mind, overriding generations of ingrained caution, overriding the fear born from the Great Mistake and the trauma of past encounters. Trust the unique energy signature. Trust the light that answered mine. Trust her. "Keket," I began, the name feeling both intimate and momentous on my tongue, my voice striving for the calm gravitas expected of my station, even as my internal rhythm faltered, a counterpoint to the steady hum of the crystal. "Your journeys... they sing of realms beyond my people's wildest imaginings, of a universe I have only known through fragmented lore and distant light." The words felt clumsy, inadequate to convey the depth of my fascination, the intellectual pull she exerted. "Allow me to offer a counterpoint. Perhaps... a harmony of worlds?" Was I offering harmony, or inviting a dangerous dissonance that could shatter everything my ancestors had built? The fear flickered, unwelcome, a cold whisper against the warmth her presence ignited. I pushed it, focusing on potential, on hope. "Extend your sojourn, Keket. Come. Witness the Kryll heart. My city. Home". Offering entry felt like offering a piece of my own being, laid bare, vulnerable, a trust I had extended to no outsider in my lifetime.

Her thoughtful silence stretched, amplifying the cave's soft hum, amplifying my own internal tension. I watched her, watching those intelligent green eyes studying the shimmering energy veil concealing the city entrance, her Terran mind undoubtedly analyzing, calculating risks, assessing the formidable barrier. Then she turned that penetrating gaze on me, and I felt the full weight of her attention.

"Your city... shielded by this formidable energy?" Pride surged, hot and fierce – our ingenuity, our survival manifested in that shimmering barrier, a testament to our resilience. Cold dread pooled beneath it, the ever-present fear of its vulnerability. "Indeed," I affirmed, the word echoing slightly in the vast space. I consciously straightened, drawing on the public persona, the image of the unwavering Protector. "Woven from Xylos's soul, a symphony of crystal energy and ancient lore, amplified by the Heartstone." A necessity born from terror, the memory whispered, a monument to loss, a constant reminder of the Great Mistake. I needed her to see the strength, the beauty, not the deep vulnerability it represented, not the patched section of the shield visible only to Kryll senses. "It has safeguarded our lineage for epochs, a sanctuary built on the lessons of the past." I held her gaze, hoping she saw confidence, not the desperate plea churning beneath, hoping she saw the value of what we protected. My pulse thrummed a frantic rhythm against the shield's steady, powerful hum.

A childish urge surged – reach out, take her hand, feel the solid reassurance of her physical presence, anchor myself to her reality – warring fiercely with ingrained caution, with the imperative of self-preservation learned through painful history, with the ancient warnings against uncontrolled resonance. Taking a steadying breath, focusing my will, I extended my own energy towards the veil, merging my signature with its familiar matrix, a part of the shield's very being. I felt the familiar pressure as the shield assessed her, its resonant vibration deepening, modulating strangely as it interacted with the unique starlight signature clinging to her, emanating from her amplified systems. A flicker of resistance, a query from the ancient energy, then... acceptance.

The veil rippled, parting with a soft whoosh that felt unnervingly like the shield itself exhaling a held breath, granting passage. Light spilled out, brilliant, multifaceted, illuminating the sharp, beautiful lines of her face, transforming her features with its ethereal glow. Stepping through felt irrevocable. I had opened the door. There was no closing it now, whatever the consequences, whatever waited on the other side of this threshold.

Her reaction was immediate, visceral. A soft gasp, her eyes widening – pure, unadulterated wonder transforming her usually guarded features, a raw, genuine awe that resonated deep within me. Possessive pride washed over me, fierce and grounding. Yes. See it. See what we are. What we protect. See the beauty that justifies the sacrifice. But even as I savored her awe, a colder, analytical part of me surfaced, a whisper of the ancient fear. Was there a flicker of scientific assessment beneath the wonder? Was she cataloging energy signatures, architectural stress points, potential resources even now, seeing only data where I saw soul? The old wound, the betrayal by past off-worlders seeking to exploit Xylos, throbbed faintly. Who are you, Keket, truly, behind those star-filled eyes? Are you the hope I dare to believe, or the echo of the past I fear?

I walked beside her along the opalescent pathway, the city's glow reflecting warmly on her dark skin, making her seem both radiant and utterly, fundamentally alien in this context. The city hummed around us, a familiar lullaby of contained power and life, but heard differently now, beside her – the constant vigilance woven into the harmony felt starker, the power more immense, the isolation more profound. I remembered running these paths as a child, dreaming of the very stars she navigated so casually, of the worlds she had seen. Now, a piece of that distant dream walked beside me, tangible, magnetic, intensely real, a living embodiment of the universe I had only imagined.

The urge to close the small distance between us was a physical ache, a pull that defied logic and protocol. Maintain decorum, Zephyr. She is a guest. An unknown quantity. My heart hammered a rhythm entirely at odds with my attempted composure, a frantic beat against the steady pulse of the city. Rounding a spire carved from rose quartz, the air shimmered, light pooling strangely. An energy fluctuation? A ripple in the shield? The Path beneath her foot... shifted, buckled slightly, a minor instability in the ancient energy flow. Before I could fully analyze the anomaly, she cried out softly, stumbling, her balance lost.

Instinct obliterated protocol. Thought dissolved. My hand shot out, finding hers, catching her before she fell. For a fraction of a second before skin met skin, awareness suspended – the boundary, the implications, the legends warning against uncontrolled resonance, the fear of the Unraveling – then contact. Not just warmth. Not electricity. Connection. A circuit snapping shut with impossible force, bridging Terran and Kryll, technology and biology, starlight and planetary core. A feeling of rightness, of a missing piece clicking into place, profound and utterly terrifying in its power.

The universe screamed. Not merely light, though light exploded behind my eyes, a blinding, chaotic supernova of sensation. Sound – a thousand crystals shattering and reforming in a deafening chord that resonated in my bones, in the very structure of the city. Pressure – my mind cracking open, vulnerable, exposed to the raw vastness she carried within her, the relentless drive, the sharp intelligence, the deep-seated loneliness. Her amplified systems blazed like captured supernovae, raw starlight flooding my senses, overwhelming my own energy field. My own energy patterns erupted in uncontrolled response, searing lines of green and violet light flashing across my skin, agony and ecstasy indistinguishable, a fusion of pain and power.

Vision became violent immersion. Nebulae swirled, magnificent, terrifyingly chaotic, rife with destructive beauty, the raw energy of creation.

I felt the crushing, empty cold of the void she traveled daily, the burning fury of star-birth, the raw, untamed energies her Watcher senses navigated. Fleeting images assaulted me – the tormented face of my ancestor during the Great Mistake, crying out as the Path fractured, as the Unraveling began; a cold, analytical thought, perhaps from her AI, evaluating my capabilities even in this maelstrom of shared consciousness; the fragile image of her ship, the Celestial Barque, adrift and alone in the crushing darkness between suns, a small point of light against the overwhelming blackness. Harmony and chaos. Creation and destruction. My mind collided with hers, terrifying, exhilarating, an intermingling where boundaries blurred – where did Zephyr end and Keket begin? Was this the resonance the prophecies spoke of? The Nexus Path potential unleashed? Was this connection... or annihilation?

Abruptly, as quickly as it began, it snapped back. My Kryll senses solidified, sharp-edged, almost painfully real, returning to the familiar, grounding reality of my own body, my own world. I instinctively ripped my hand from hers, recoiling as if struck by lightning, needing distance, needing to re-establish the boundaries that had just been annihilated. Gasping, struggling to pull air into suddenly tight lungs, the lingering warmth on my palm felt like the imprint of her very soul, a brand against my skin. I stared at her, seeing the same shock, the same dawning terror mirrored in her wide green eyes, the vibrant green now clouded with fear and confusion.

This wasn't just interaction. It was a maelstrom. A power unleashed, perhaps unwisely, irrevocably. It answered nothing, yet irrevocably changed everything. My carefully constructed world, my harmony, my very self, had just been exposed to the wild, unpredictable, utterly overwhelming star symphony she carried within her amplified being. This connection, this Path she had unknowingly touched... it was real. And I knew, with chilling certainty, nothing would ever be the same. A primal alarm, echoing a terror older than his own memories, screamed through his being – the chilling signature of off-world intrusion, a sound his ancestors had last heard during the Unraveling. Something was alerted. Something shifted. The very energy of Xylos felt... watched. The ancient texts spoke of 'Silent Watchers Beyond'. Had we just announced our presence?

I saw the profound exhaustion settling over her features then, the adrenaline finally draining away, leaving behind the bone-deep weariness of someone who had touched the infinite and barely survived the recoil. The slight tremor in her hands, the way she unconsciously rubbed her temples – signs of overload clear even across the species divide. The connection, the revelations, the inherent danger of our situation... it demanded rest. Secure rest.

"Keket," I said, softening my tone, deliberately stepping back from the intensity of the Path revelations. "What we experienced... it takes a toll. On mind, body, energy field." My own systems felt frayed, echoing with phantom sensations. "Further discussion now, while we are depleted, serves little purpose. You require restoration. Privacy." She looked hesitant, her ingrained vigilance warring with undeniable fatigue. "My crew..." "Are safe aboard their vessel," I assured her quickly. "They will be monitored, but undisturbed unless you direct otherwise. But you... you need sanctuary." I made a decision, diverging from standard protocol for accommodating off-worlders, which typically involved designated guest wings far from the central spire's core. This felt... different. Necessary. "Come. There is a place nearby. Secure. Quiet." I led her away from the echoing vastness of the plaza, through corridors that pulsed with the city's soft, internal light. I noted the way she moved, still graceful but with an underlying stiffness, her senses likely still overwhelmed by the alien architecture and energy fields even without the Path's direct influence. Having her here, walking these paths usually reserved for Kryll council or high-ranking protectors, felt strange, unprecedented, yet undeniably... right. Protectiveness warred with the strategic implications. We arrived before a seamless section of crystalline wall near the upper levels of the command spire, integrated organically into the structure. Placing my palm upon it, I channeled a specific energy signature. The wall shimmered, then dilated silently inward, revealing not the expected corridor, but a self-contained suite. "This is a Solitude Chamber," I explained, gesturing to her inside. "Used rarely. For deep meditation, recovery from significant energy expenditure, or... ensuring absolute privacy for sensitive matters. It is shielded, isolated from the main city network. You will be undisturbed here." I wouldn't admit it was also one of the most secure locations within the spire, shielded even from most internal Kryll sensors. I watched her step hesitantly across the threshold, her green eyes taking in the unfamiliar space. I felt a strange reluctance to leave her, a pull to stay, to ensure her comfort, but knew that space was what she needed most now. "Rest, Keket. Sustenance will be provided. We face the larger implications... when you are restored." With a final, lingering look, I signaled the door to close, sealing her within the sanctuary, the echo of her starlight energy leaving a tangible void in the corridor behind me.

Chapter 9: Fractured Calm

Keket

Lungs burned, dragging ragged breaths that tasted metallic. Charged. Like the air before a lightning strike on a high-atmosphere station. Or the air in the lower habs during the outbreak. The crystal city snapped back into sharp, painful focus around me. Jarringly solid after the swirling, non-Euclidean chaos of... whatever that cataclysmic connection had been. My hand – the one he'd held, the one that had become a conduit for universes – tingled violently. Simultaneously freezing cold and searing hot. Nerve endings screaming contradictory signals. Echoes of shattering light, impossible cosmic vistas, and raw, alien emotion reverberated behind my eyelids, refusing to fade. Leaving a psychic residue that felt like grit in my mind. Disorientation was a physical weight. The glowing opalescent path tilting nauseatingly beneath my boots. My internal chronometer felt fractured. Time itself momentarily warped, stretched, then snapped back.

I stumbled back another step, needing precious distance. Needing to re-establish the boundary that had just been annihilated. Ripped away without my consent. Control, Keket. Regain control. Training screamed. A thin, frayed lifeline in the torrent of sensation and incomprehensible emotion that threatened to drown me. Years in the Collective, navigating complex systems, hostile negotiations, the dangers of the void – none of it had prepared me for this violation. This forced intimacy. The energy surge from his touch. From our bond. It hadn't just shown me things; it had ripped through every mental shield, every layer of command discipline I possessed. It had opened my mind to his, and his to mine, with brutal, unasked-for honesty.

My fingers, still shaky but finding purpose, went to the subtle interface point behind my ear, activating my internal bio-monitors. Data streams, usually a comfort, now seemed alien. Flashing off-the-charts synaptic activity, cortisol spikes, and anomalous energy resonance patterns my implants struggled to even classify. Ma'at would need these sensor logs, the bio-readings... Gods, my cold, analytical brain felt ridiculously inadequate. Trying to catalogue a supernova with a hand lens. I forced my spine straight, smoothed the front of my uniform tunic with trembling fingers – a useless, reflexive gesture of normalcy in the face of utter abnormality. A desperate attempt to project a composure I didn't feel. Don't look at him. Analyze the event. Massive bio-electric discharge, clearly. Sympathetic energy exchange triggered by physical contact in proximity to a potent energy source – the crystals, the city's core? – amplified catastrophically by my integrated systems interacting with his unknown Kryll biology. Resulting in a shared hallucinatory state? Induced telepathic overlay? The terms felt clinical, sterile, utterly insufficient to describe the raw, shattering experience.

But it wasn't just energy. It wasn't just data. It was... intimacy. Terrifying, unsought intimacy. I felt... him. His shock mirroring mine, yes, but beneath it, glimpses... a deep-seated loneliness resonating like a cold star. The crushing weight of his responsibility for this world. A fierce protective pride for this place he called heart... and stranger still, a flicker of undeniable awe directed not just at the universe I represented, but specifically, confusingly, at me. It was the feeling of being utterly exposed. His vulnerability laid bare, his history, his burdens, his loneliness, his fierce pride for this hidden world. And terrifyingly, *my* own self laid bare to him. My relentless determination, the ever-present hum of duty that was both shield and cage, the sharp edges of solitude honed by long voyages between silent stars, the carefully buried fears of failure, of inadequacy, the ghost of the child in the lower habs... Exposed. Stripped bare and utterly exposed to this alien warrior by a simple touch. My carefully constructed internal walls are crumbling around me. How could I, officer of the Sah Collective, reconcile this with this when my mind had been forcibly intertwined with an alien warrior? The intimacy was a violation, yes, but beneath the terror, a horrifying, undeniable whisper of... belonging. Of being seen in a way no one, not even herself, had ever managed. It was a weakness, a catastrophic vulnerability, and yet, the most compelling mystery I had ever encountered. My mind, usually a fortress of calculated data and strategic projections, felt like a breached hull. And my crew, orbiting above in blissful ignorance, depended on that fortress holding. The thought was a cold, sharp anchor, dragging me back from the edge of the abyss that had just opened within me.

My breath hitched again, bordering on hyperventilation. No. I couldn't fall apart here, not in this alien city, not under that intense, assessing gaze. Duty. Mission. Crew. My crew. Waiting in orbit, trusting me, depending on my stability. The thought was an anchor, dragging me back from the edge of the abyss that had just opened in my mind. My fingers, still shaky but finding purpose, subtly tapped the command sequence behind my ear again, activating the secure internal comm embedded within my implants, bypassing the open city network. Minimal subvocalization required. "Barque Actual, status report". My voice was a low murmur, hopefully unnoticed by Zephyr, who still seemed to be gathering himself several feet away, processing the psychic fallout, his back half-turned to me.

Lieutenant Joric's calm, steady voice instantly filled my mind. Blessedly normal. Blessedly real. A lifeline to the world I understood. "All systems green, Captain. Orbit stable. No external contacts detected. We registered minor, localized atmospheric energy fluctuations near your projected position approximately two minutes ago, rapidly dissipating now. Anything to report?". Minor fluctuations. Right. Like a fusion core breach is a 'small heat variance'. The sheer understatement was almost darkly comical, highlighting the vast gulf between their reality and the one I had just experienced. But the data point itself... external confirmation. The ship's sensors had picked it up. Whatever happened, it wasn't just in our heads. It was real. And it had an external impact.

"Negative, Lieutenant. Environmental anomaly," I lied, the deception feeling necessary, protective. How could I even begin to explain? How could I articulate seeing nebulae bloom behind a stranger's eyes? "Maintain standard watch protocols. Keket out".

The connection severed, leaving me alone again in the vibrating silence of the plaza, punctuated only by the city's soft, pervasive hum and the suddenly too-loud, frantic drumming of my own heartbeat. They're fine. Relief was sharp, almost painful in its intensity. My crew was safe. The Celestial Barque, my other home, my sphere of control and responsibility, was holding steady in orbit. Reality existed up there, solid, dependable, governed by physics I understood – a stark, nauseating contrast to the chaos within me, the sheer impossibility of what had just transpired down here. Guilt twisted in my gut, a sour taste in my mouth. Down here, mesmerized by glowing caves, distracted by a striking alien warrior – don't go there, Keket – and then completely losing control during an inexplicable energy backlash... while my crew waited above, relying on my command, my stability, my unwavering focus. How could I reconcile the Captain they needed, the capable officer who navigated the void, with the woman whose knees still felt weak, whose mind was reeling from seeing universes unfold through another's consciousness, whose carefully constructed defenses had just been breached on a fundamental level? This connection, this vulnerability... it wasn't just personal; it was a tactical liability. What if it happened again? What if it could be triggered remotely, used against me, against my crew?

Beyond the immediate physical and emotional fallout, my enhanced senses began to pick up subtle shifts in the city's ambient energy hum. A faint, high-frequency static seemed layered beneath the familiar resonance of the crystals. It wasn't the steady pulse of Xylos, or the structured energy of the city's systems. It felt... alien. Like a distant, unfamiliar signal had been activated. Or attracted. Was this an echo of the Path experience? A consequence of our uncontrolled connection? The vague warnings from my calibration about 'unraveling light' and 'currents that bite' flickered in my mind, laced now with a fresh, chilling dread. This connection felt tied to something ancient, something potentially dangerous, something that resonated with the buried fears I'd glimpsed in Zephyr.

I finally risked looking directly at Zephyr again. He had regained some composure, drawing himself up with that quiet intensity, the warrior's mask beginning to settle back into place, though the shock hadn't fully faded from his eyes. If anything, it had deepened into something else – a raw awareness, an intensity that pinned me in place, demanding my attention. He wasn't just looking at me anymore; he was looking into me, searching for the echoes of that shared, cataclysmic moment. And I realized, with a jolt unrelated to any energy discharge, I was doing the exact same thing, searching his face for answers I couldn't articulate. Because beneath the fear, beneath the violation of forced intimacy, something else stubbornly persisted, a strange, unsettling counterpoint to the chaos. Fascination, yes, but more than that. A fleeting, terrifying sense of having been seen, truly seen, understood on a level that transcended language, science, species... and it was horrifyingly, undeniably attractive in its raw authenticity. He was no longer just an enigmatic alien leader, an obstacle or key to the mission. He was the other half of this impossible equation, the being whose touch had unlocked something ancient or alien within my amplified systems, something overwhelming within myself.

He opened his mouth, then closed it, seemingly struggling for words, his throat working. Finally, he spoke, my name a rough sound on his alien tongue, heavy with everything unspoken, everything felt between us. "Keket...". Just the name. It hung in the air between us, annihilating the comfortable diplomat/ captain distance, the careful alien/human boundary. We were two beings, caught in the fragile, unnerving space after an explosion, breathing the fallout, bound by a shared experience that defied logic and protocol. The city's hum felt distant, muted by the roar in my ears, the frantic beat of my own heart slowly starting to calm. Zephyr was still standing meters away, a silhouette against the soft, alien light, his chest heaving with ragged breaths that mirrored my own. The psychic echoes of the Path, of collapsing realities and ancient fears, still clawed at the edges of my mind, leaving me feeling raw and exposed. More exposed than I'd felt since the Cerulean Plague outbreak, when the air itself had felt like a violation.

I took a shaky step towards him, driven by an instinct I couldn't name – a desperate need for something solid, something real, in the wake of touching the infinite and finding it terrifying. His luminous eyes, wide and searching, locked onto mine, and I saw my own shock, my own bewildered fear, reflected in their depths. He took a step too, closing the distance between us until he was just within reach. The air between us crackled, not with residual Path energy, but with a different kind of charge, thick and heavy with unspoken understanding.

My hand trembled as I lifted it, not towards my comm or a weapon, but towards him. Towards the intricate, glowing patterns on his arm, mirroring the alien light that had erupted from my own tech. He didn't flinch. He just watched my hand rise, his gaze unwavering. When my trembling fingertips, still faintly buzzing with residual energy, brushed against the smooth, surprisingly warm skin of his forearm, it wasn't the explosive surge from before, but a jolt of pure warmth, grounding, anchoring. His hand came up then, covering mine, his fingers long and strong, calloused in places I hadn't noticed before. He gently laced our fingers together, his rougher pads a perfect contrast to my softer ones. His thumb brushed lightly, almost reverently, over the back of my hand, stroking a path over the sensitive skin there. The simple touch sent a deep shiver down my spine, chasing away the lingering echoes of cosmic chaos, replacing them with a purely physical awareness that anchored me firmly in the present. There were no star charts for this, no Collective protocols to follow.

Mission, duty, carefully constructed control... all felt terrifyingly fragile against the undeniable, complex, dangerously compelling pull of the connection now thrumming, volatile and unpredictable, between us.

Chapter 10: Whispers Through the Static

Zephyr

Xylos's crystalline light, usually a soothing balm, felt harsh now. Grating against nerves rubbed raw by the psychic detonation between us. The city's familiar ambient hum was a discordant vibration against the echo of shattering stars still ringing in the hollow spaces of my mind. Air shuddered in my lungs, thick with the lingering scent of her energy – ozone, distant stars, and something uniquely, indefinably Keket. My hand, the one that had seized hers in that blinding moment of pure instinct, felt strangely empty, yet burned with the phantom imprint of her touch. Cellular memory of that violent, consuming connection. It had bypassed every defense.

The visions assaulted my waking thoughts – the terrifying, chaotic beauty of nebulae I'd only glimpsed in ancient Kryll star-lore; the crushing, soul-deep cold of the void she navigated as casually as I walked these crystal paths; the stark, remembered fear in my own ancestor's eyes during the Great Mistake, a face contorted in agony as the Path fractured; her ship, the Celestial Barque, impossibly small and terrifyingly alone in the crushing darkness between suns... It was too much. An entire universe, vast and indifferent, had poured into me through her hand, through the conduit our combined energies had unwittingly forged. And amidst the cosmic storm, the feeling of her mind against mine – sharp, relentless, yet holding a core of fierce loyalty and deep-seated loneliness. I had felt her history, the weight of expectations, the constant hum of duty she carried like armor, the stark reality of the "ground static" she fled. Seeing her vulnerability, her yearning for something more real... it resonated with a part of me I rarely acknowledged.

I forced myself to look at her across the opalescent expanse of the plaza where we stood frozen. Even amidst the crystalline splendor of my home, she remained the most arresting sight – tall for her species, sculpted by shadows and light, her dark skin absorbing the city's ethereal glow. Her long locs, usually neatly contained, were slightly disturbed, framing a face etched with the same profound shock that surely marked my own. But it was her eyes – those impossible, searching green eyes, portals to the star-filled void she called home – that held me captive, wide now with a fear and bewildered wonder that mirrored the tempest raging inside my own chest. The faint blue light pulsing along the intricate pathways tracing her neck and arm seemed like captured starlight, a living map of the cosmos she carried within her very being. Seeing her so undone, stripped bare of the Captain's composure, so vulnerable... it sparked something deep within me, something far beyond the duty of a protector – a fierce, almost painful urge to shield her, to draw her back from the precipice of the infinite we had just glimpsed. My carefully constructed walls, built on generations of isolation and caution, felt paper-thin against this wave of protective instinct.

"Zephyr," she murmured, her voice husky, rough from the overload, the sound of my name on her Terran lips sending an unexpected tremor through my carefully controlled systems. It sounded less like a query, more like an anchor desperately sought in the chaos. "What... What was that? What are we seeing?"

What had we seen? What abyss had we brushed against? "Ourselves, I think," I managed, my own voice rougher, deeper than intended, the carefully cultivated calm of the warrior feeling distant, utterly irrelevant now. "Pieces of each other. Echoes." How could I articulate the feeling of her loneliness, that sharp, crystalline edge of solitude honed by countless light-years traveling the empty dark? The feeling resonated sickeningly with the isolation inherent in my own position, a burden I rarely acknowledged. "Your stars... Keket, I felt the cold, the crushing loneliness of your journeys. But also... the fire. The relentless determination that drives you." My voice filled with an awe I didn't try to hide, the sheer scale of her existence overwhelming my ingrained Kryll reserve. "It was... immense."

"And I saw your history," she countered softly, her gaze holding mine tenaciously, refusing to look away despite the raw, shattering intimacy of the exchange. "The weight you carry for this place. The fear... the memory of fire and pain... but also such fierce pride." She paused, her voice dropping, mirroring my own awe. "I felt... your connection. To all of this." That fragile understanding, spun between us in the wreckage of our composure, felt more real, more substantial, than the enduring crystal beneath my feet.

An undeniable pull radiated from her. A gravity stronger than Xylos's own. Threatening to unravel the careful balance I had maintained my entire life. I took an involuntary step towards her, closing the distance, needing... what?

Reassurance? Contact? To confirm the reality of her presence after touching the void through her mind? As I moved, my arm brushed against hers, the surprisingly yielding fabric of her uniform against my bare skin.

Flash. Not the violent surge from before. This was... softer. Quieter. A wave of warmth. A whisper of connection. Focused and clear. For an instant, the soaring crystal city dissolved, and I was seeing through her eyes again – the cool, grey, sterile lines of her metal world, the endless starfield beckoning outside a viewport, feeling the familiar cage of its walls and her restless spirit yearning, aching, for the dark beyond, for the purpose she hadn't yet found. It was a glimpse into the gilded cage she flew from, a confinement utterly alien to my experience, yet the yearning felt achingly familiar. I saw her flinch simultaneously, gasp softly, her green eyes widening as she, presumably, glimpsed something of my own world through my senses – perhaps the weight of the Falls, the scent of the crystal gardens.

We pulled back, but not with the panicked speed of before. There was a shared breath, a hesitation, the space between our arms tingling, alive with residual energy. Her gaze locked on mine, searching, questioning. "Did you...?"

"Yes," I breathed, the single word encompassing the impossible reality we now shared. And in that moment of shared, secondary sight, the ancient pieces slammed into place within my mind with the force of revelation. The fragmented legends the Elders guarded so closely. The prophecies of the 'Nexus Path,' dismissed by many as cautionary myths after the Great Mistake. The dormant power residing in the First Light lineage – my lineage – waiting, waiting for the catalyst, the counterpart from the stars whose unique energy signature, whose amplified starlight, would complete the circuit. The Ky'lora. The Mate. Not just a partner in lineage, but the literal key, the specific resonant frequency needed to unlock the paths between worlds, a power sealed away in terror after the catastrophe of the Great Mistake.

It wasn't just a connection. It was the connection. She, Keket, Captain of the Celestial Barque, traveler from the void, daughter of the Watchers, bearer of starlight... she was the one spoken of in hushed, fearful tones for centuries. The realization struck me with the force of a physical blow, stealing the air from my lungs. This Terran woman, with her impossible green eyes that held the fire of distant suns and a vulnerability that mirrored his own hidden aches, wasn't just a catalyst; she was destiny. The Ky'lora. His Mate. The ancient texts, the half-forgotten prophecies, the very pulse of Xylos beneath his feet – it all coalesced into this single, staggering truth. And the fierce, possessive protectiveness that surged through him had little to do with lineage or planetary survival, and everything to do with the woman whose starlight had answered his soul's deepest shadow.

A fierce, possessive protectiveness surged through me, so intense, so absolute, it was almost painful. My lineage, my people, our future, the safeguarding of Xylos itself – it was all inextricably tied to her. To this Terran woman standing before me, looking so lost amidst the alien splendor of my city, yet radiating an inner strength, a core of fire, that called to something ancient and fundamental within me. She was the missing harmony, the starlight needed to complete Xylos's song, the catalyst for a power that could save us or destroy us all.

And with that realization came a chilling dread. The violent surge. The sudden, uncontrolled glimpse into the Path. It wasn't just a revelation of our bond. It was a *disturbance*. Ancient texts warned of 'Silent Watchers Beyond'. Beings who resided within the Path's currents. Did our chaotic activation... *alert* them? Had we changed something fundamental about the Path, about Xylos, by unlocking this connection so violently? The very air of the city felt different now, subtly charged with something I couldn't identify. A low-frequency hum beneath the familiar resonance of the crystals. Unsettling. Like distant eyes had just turned towards our world.

I had to explain. Part of it, at least. The full truth – the mating bond, the biological imperative, the completion of my lineage tied directly and irrevocably to her – felt like too much, too soon. A weight she wasn't ready for, revealed in the aftermath of such trauma. It would sound like a cage, a demand, a theft of the very agency she valued. Looking at her wide, startled eyes, the vulnerability stark beneath the Captain's façade, I couldn't do that to her. Not yet. I couldn't make her feel trapped by destiny before she even understood the landscape of this new reality. Withholding this felt like a betrayal, a dangerous gamble, setting up a potential future conflict, a 'black moment' born of my own fear, yet it felt necessary for her immediate stability.

"Keket," I began again, my voice deliberately low and steady, fighting to convey reassurance I didn't entirely feel, needing to anchor her before she fractured completely. I reached out, my fingers finding the curve of her elbow, needing the physical contact, the anchor of her solid presence in the face of cosmic uncertainty. The soft jolt that passed between us was familiar now, less frightening, more like a shared current.

"This connection... It's more than energy, Keket. Far more. It's... significant." I held her gaze, willing her to see the partial truth in my eyes, praying it would be enough for now. "Ancient Kryll legends spoke of this. A merging of Xylos's heart-song, amplified through the Weaving Crystals, with the light from a distant star. A specific resonance." I focused on the shared phenomenon, the power itself, sidestepping the deeply personal implication. "That flash... the first surge, and the echo just now... it wasn't just memory or empathy. It was... elsewhere. Elsewhen, perhaps. The legends called it the 'Nexus Path'. A potential to truly... see beyond."

I saw the struggle on her face – the trained officer, the scientist, battling the undeniable evidence of her senses. "I believe," I continued, my grip tightening instinctively, protectively, grounding both of us, "that we, together, Keket, are the key to it. Our... resonance... it opens these windows." The awe I felt was real, immense, but it was centered now entirely on her, on the impossible, staggering fact of her existence and what she represented for my world, for myself. "This ability... the Path... it's why the crystals you seek, the Scarabite-7, are likely so important. They are amplifiers. Anchors. Perhaps even the conduits for this Path."

Her mind was clearly racing, grappling with the impossible implications. "Travel... between realities?" she whispered, the words barely audible, laced with disbelief and dawning fear. "It's... impossible."

"Is it?" I countered gently, holding her gaze steadfastly. "You felt it. I felt you." I saw the flicker of acknowledgment in her eyes, the memory of the shared glimpse confirming my words even as her Terran logic fought desperately against them.

"If this is real..." she breathed, looking around the glowing city as if seeing it anew, a place now charged with terrifying, limitless potential. "My mission... your city's safety... Zephyr, what does this mean?"

The weight of it settled heavily on my shoulders, heavier than the mantle of leadership had ever felt. The daughter of stars, the prophesied catalyst, the key to my people's lost power and potentially their destruction, standing vulnerable and reeling in the heart of my hidden world. "It means," I said slowly, my voice resonating with a fierce resolve I hadn't known I possessed, born of certainty and terror and undeniable connection, "that everything has changed." I met her troubled green eyes, making a silent, absolute vow I couldn't yet voice aloud. "And that I will not let this connection, or this place, or the powers that covet them, bring you harm." The words felt absolute, a truth deeper than prophecy, rooted in the undeniable gravity pulling me towards the woman whose starlight had answered the heart-song of my world across the silent void.

I saw the profound exhaustion settling over her features then, the adrenaline finally draining away, leaving behind the bone-deep weariness of someone who had touched the infinite and barely survived the recoil. The slight tremor in her hands, the way she unconsciously rubbed her temples – signs of overload clear even across the species divide. The connection, the revelations, the inherent danger of our situation... it demanded rest. Secure rest.

"Keket," I said, softening my tone, deliberately stepping back from the intensity of the Path revelations. "What we experienced... it takes a toll. On mind, body, energy field." My own systems felt frayed, echoing with phantom sensations. "Further discussion now, while we are depleted, serves little purpose. You require restoration. Privacy." She looked hesitant, her ingrained vigilance warring with undeniable fatigue. "My crew..." "Are safe aboard their vessel," I assured her quickly. "They will be monitored, but undisturbed unless you direct otherwise. But you... you need sanctuary." I made a decision, diverging from standard protocol for accommodating off-worlders, which typically involved designated guest wings far from the central spire's core. This felt... different. Necessary. "Come. There is a place nearby. Secure. Quiet." I led her away from the echoing vastness of the plaza, through corridors that pulsed with the city's soft, internal light. I noted the way she moved, still graceful but with an underlying stiffness, her senses likely still overwhelmed by the alien architecture and energy fields even without the Path's direct influence. Having her here, walking these paths usually reserved for Kryll council or high-ranking protectors, felt strange, unprecedented, yet undeniably... right. Protectiveness warred with the strategic implications. We arrived before a seamless section of crystalline wall near the upper levels of the command spire, integrated organically into the structure. Placing my palm upon it, I channeled a specific energy signature. The wall shimmered, then dilated silently inward, revealing not the expected corridor, but a self-contained suite. "This is a Solitude

Chamber," I explained, gesturing to her inside. "Used rarely. For deep meditation, recovery from significant energy expenditure, or... ensuring absolute privacy for sensitive matters. It is shielded, isolated from the main city network. You will be undisturbed here." I wouldn't admit it was also one of the most secure locations within the spire, shielded even from most internal Kryll sensors. I watched her step hesitantly across the threshold, her green eyes taking in the unfamiliar space. I felt a strange reluctance to leave her, a pull to stay, to ensure her comfort, but knew that space was what she needed most now. "Rest, Keket. Sustenance will be provided. We face the larger implications... when you are restored." With a final, lingering look, I signaled the door to close, sealing her within the sanctuary, the echo of her starlight energy leaving a tangible void in the corridor behind me.

Chapter 11: Anchored Light and Calculated Risks

Keket

The next cycle dawned, or rather, the ambient light within the Xylos Prime Spire shifted subtly from the deep violets of its designated 'night' phase to warmer golds and pale blues. Sleep had been a shallow, restless affair. Haunted by the echoes of the Nexus Path – the terrifying intimacy of shared minds, the glimpse of cosmic vastness, and the heavy weight of Zephyr's revelations about Scarabite-7's consumption and the ancient warnings from Chapter 8 and 10. Now, washed, clad in a fresh uniform that felt inadequate armor against the spire's alien elegance and the day's unknown challenges, I braced myself for the formal invitation Zephyr had extended for 'morning sustenance' – brunch, essentially – not just for me, but for my senior officers. A calculated gesture of alliance after yesterday's turmoil, demanding careful navigation and a performance of Collective composure.

The dining space was high in the spire, vast yet intimate. Overlooking the glowing expanse of the city through a seamless, curved crystalline wall that seemed to dissolve the boundary between inside and out. Light danced across a polished table that seemed grown from the floor, adorned with bowls of vibrant, unidentifiable fruits and steaming carafes emitting complex, alien aromas. Zephyr was already there, sans armor today, dressed in flowing robes of deep emerald that emphasized his height and the quiet authority he carried. He greeted us with a formal inclination of his head, his luminous green eyes assessing each of my crew members as they entered. A silent evaluation that missed nothing. Lingering for a fraction longer on me.

"Welcome," Zephyr's resonant voice filled the space, warmer than the formal tone he'd used on the comm, yet still holding the weight of command. "Please, partake. Xylos offers unique sustenance. We are grateful you accepted our invitation."

The meal was another sensory exploration – tangy purple berries that fizzed lightly on the tongue, warm, bread-like fungi with a savory, almost meaty flavor, juices that changed color as you drank them, shifting from pale gold to deep crimson. Conversation was stilted initially, a dance between Terran pragmatism and Kryll philosophy, filtered through Ma'at's seamless translation woven into my neural interface, allowing me to understand Zephyr's melodic clicks and whistles as clear language.

Bastet, predictably, was the first to break the polite silence with a technical query, her curiosity overriding caution. "Commander Zephyr," she began, gesturing towards the glowing walls, a mixture of awe and skepticism on her face, "the energy regulation required for stable bioluminescence on this scale, integrated with structural support... The materials science alone is fascinating. Are the primary conduits crystal-based or—"

"The spire lives, Chief Engineer Bastet," Zephyr interrupted gently, though a flicker of amusement touched his eyes, appreciating her directness. "It grows according to energy flows directed by conscious intent and ancient harmonics. Less engineering, more... cultivation. The conduits are extensions of the Heartstone's energy field, guided by the city's consciousness."

Bastet blinked, her Terran engineering brain clearly struggling to process a concept that defied her training. "Cultivation," she repeated faintly, looking at the wall as if it might sprout a new wing or demand fertilizer, a clear note of professional unease in her voice. "Remarkable. And... stable?" Zephyr's expression remained composed, but I saw the subtle tightening around his mouth. "It has endured for epochs," he replied, his tone firm...

"Remarkable. And... stable?" Bastet repeated, her brow furrowed, her Terran engineering brain clearly struggling to process a concept that defied her training, her voice tinged with professional unease. "Sir, with all due respect, systems I can't quantify, materials that 'grow' rather than being constructed with predictable tensile strength... it feels fundamentally unstable. Like something that could decide to cease functioning if its power source is... disrupted." She paused, glancing subtly towards me, a shared understanding of the Scarabite-7 drain revealed adding an unspoken layer to her concern. "I don't trust tech, I can't isolate and understand. This 'cultivation,' Zephyr's term, felt like a philosophical divide made physical, highlighting the gap between Terran control and Kryll symbiosis.

Sekem, ever practical, spoke next. "Commander, the atmospheric composition is within our suit parameters, but the density is significant. What are the primary atmospheric components? And the biological markers our probes detected... are they hazardous to Terran life?"

"The atmosphere is primarily nitrogen and oxygen, similar to Old Earth, but with higher concentrations of trace minerals and bio-energetic particles," Zephyr explained, his gaze shifting to Sekem, acknowledging his concern for the crew's safety. "The flora and fauna are intrinsically linked to Xylos's energy field. Most are not overtly hostile, but sealed protocols are recommended until further analysis. Some bio-resonant frequencies can be... disorienting to uncalibrated senses."

Joric, his eyes scanning the room, focused on a different aspect. "Commander, our long-range scans detected energy modulations around the city perimeter that didn't match the main shield harmonics. Are there... other energy sources? Or perhaps... internal security systems operating independently?" His question was pointed, hinting at the subtle energy anomalies I'd perceived earlier. The energy signatures of the Kryll who had emerged with Zephyr, their different energy patterns, hinted at divisions. This now suggested more formal, *independent* systems – potentially tied to different factions.

Zephyr's expression remained composed, but I saw a flicker of something unreadable in his eyes at Joric's question, a subtle tightening around his mouth. "The city's energy field is complex, Lieutenant Joric," he replied smoothly, neither confirming nor denying. "It has many layers and redundancies. Our primary focus is defense." He deflected the question with practiced ease, a clear signal that some information remained off-limits.

I acted as the bridge, translating Bastet's technical curiosity into broader questions about Kryll philosophy regarding technology and nature, discussing the Collective's resource pressures (carefully omitting the most critical details of the bottleneck, but hinting at the worsening situation through phrases like "increasing demands" and "stretching supply lines"). I subtly brought up the unusual lack of recent high-level Collective transmissions, adding to my crew's and my own underlying tension about our isolation and the potential for the Collective to have taken drastic measures. I observed Zephyr throughout. He was a gracious host, answering our questions with a measured openness, revealing what he chose to reveal, yet his attention consistently, subtly, returned to me. Across the table, amidst the polite conversation and the alien flavors, I felt the pull – the lingering resonance of the Path, the undeniable awareness forged between us yesterday. It was a silent hum beneath the surface, a shared secret in a room full of wary observers. I caught his gaze across the table, holding it for a fraction longer than necessary, a silent acknowledgment of the connection that bound us in this strange place. He offered a subtle, almost imperceptible incline of his head in return, a private exchange in a public setting. I observed him interacting with his own people, the Kryll staff who moved with quiet grace around the dining space, noting the difference in their posture, the subtle shifts in their bioluminescent patterns as they communicated with him. He was clearly revered, a leader who inspired loyalty, but I also saw the weight he carried, the constant vigilance in his eyes even in this moment of relative peace.

It felt... significant. Frightening, yes, given its unpredictable nature and the warnings of the Great Mistake and the chilling awareness of the 'Silent Watchers Beyond' from Chapter 10, but also like finding a specific, unique frequency in the universe that only we could perceive. A shared purpose, perhaps, hidden within this galactic mystery, a counterpoint to the corporate grind I'd left behind.

As the meal concluded, Zephyr's gaze met mine across the polished crystal, serious now, the subtle shift in his demeanor signaling the transition from host to commander, from diplomacy to the task at hand. "Captain Keket. We have discussed the... phenomenon. The Nexus Path. Its potential, its danger, it's clear link to the crystals you seek – Scarabite-7, the Heartstone." He paused, letting the weight settle, the implications of my discovery about its consumption hanging in the air between us, a shared burden. "Ignoring it is not an option. Understanding it is imperative. For both our peoples, and perhaps for the safety of others."

Anticipation prickled my skin, a mix of scientific eagerness and apprehension. This was it. The next step into the unknown. But the weight of the Scarabite-7 drain, the warnings from the Path glimpse, the uncertainty about the Collective and internal Kryll dynamics... it made this next step feel like a jump into an abyss.

"I agree," I said, my voice steady, mirroring his seriousness. "We need data. Controlled parameters. A structured approach."

"Precisely," Zephyr nodded, a flicker of approval in his eyes. "I propose we proceed to the primary convergence chamber near the Heartstone formation. The legends suggest focused contact is possible there, less chaotic than our...

initial experience." He glanced briefly at me, a shared memory of shattering light and overwhelming sensation passing between us, a silent acknowledgment of the trauma and the unexpected intimacy. "With the proper anchors."

The air grew thick with unspoken understanding. Anchors. Us. Together. My crew shifted, sensing the shift in tone, the gravity of the impending task. Bastet looked ready to object on grounds of sheer physics and unknown variables, her hand already going to her datapad, but Sekem placed a subtle, steady hand on her arm, a silent reminder of chain of command and trust. They trusted my lead, even into the utterly unknown, even when it felt like I was navigating a power I barely understood, with an alien who resonated with me in impossible ways. The escalating galactic situation, the chilling possibility that our isolation wasn't just a coincidence but tied to a Collective lockdown or worse, added urgency. We couldn't afford to wait. The Scarabite-7, the Path, understanding them felt like our only path forward. It was a calculated risk. A necessary gamble.

"We're ready when you are, Commander," I said, my resolve firming. The vast chamber housing the colossal Scarabite-7 spire felt different today. Yesterday's raw shock had subsided, replaced by a focused, high-stakes tension. The great crystal pulsed with its soft, internal emerald light, seeming to breathe in rhythm with the low hum that resonated through the floor, a deep, powerful vibration that felt both ancient and alive. Zephyr stood near its base, stripped down to his harness and pants, the intricate patterns on his arms shimmering faintly, a visual echo of the spire's own internal light. The commander was present, yes, his posture radiating control, but so was the being who had shared the terrifying beauty of the void with me, whose touch had unlocked something fundamental.

"The legends are fragmented," he said, his voice lower here, almost reverent, resonating with the chamber's hum. "They speak of the Path as 'currents between realities,' of the Heartstone as the 'Wellspring.' They warn of 'drawing too deeply,' lest the 'World Shield' falter, and hint at 'Silent Watchers Beyond' disturbed by careless passage." He looked at me, the weight of millennia in his gaze, the burden of his people's history visible. "This requires absolute synchronization, Keket. Shared focus. An anchor."

Anchor. The word echoed, resonating with the memory of his hand in mine, the explosion, the subsequent controlled flash, the terrifying intimacy.

My gaze flickered to his hand, then quickly away, focusing on the technical setup, the equipment we would use. This physical contact wasn't impulse today; it was methodology, a hypothesis based on our previous chaotic interactions. A shared circuit, as I'd hypothesized, requires trust, proximity, vulnerability. My scientific mind embraced the logic, the elegant simplicity of the potential solution; the woman recoiled slightly from the dangerous intimacy it demanded, the memory of being overwhelmed still fresh. Yet, the drive to understand, to map this impossible frontier, was stronger than my apprehension. This was discovery on a scale I'd never dreamed of, a purpose far removed from optimizing corporate extraction routes. This felt... meaningful, vital, a chance to understand something truly profound. A chance that felt increasingly urgent with the growing silence from Collective space.

"We learned yesterday," I stated, meeting his gaze, pushing down the tremor of apprehension by focusing on the data, on the science, "Physical contact, shared focus, proximity to the resonant crystal. It stabilizes the connection, channels the energy. My bio-filaments, your connection to the Heartstone – they act as the necessary circuit." I checked the readings on the small console I'd brought in, calibrating the regulators, ensuring the safety overrides were active.

Zephyr nodded solemnly, confirming my analysis, a collaborative partner in this scientific endeavor. "Two resonant points," he agreed. "Your amplified Watcher senses acting as the lens, calibrated to perceive the Path's currents, my connection to the Heartstone as the source, the anchor, the power. We attempt to guide the flow, not simply be swept away." He stepped closer, the air crackling with latent energy between us, the hum of the Scarabite-7 spire intensifying. He extended his hand, palm up, a silent offering of trust and shared risk, his fingers long and strong, the patterns on his skin pulsing faintly in response to the crystal's energy, mirroring the faint glow beneath my own skin. Taking a deep breath that tasted of ozone and energized crystal and the unique, grounding scent of him, I met his gaze and placed my hand in his, my fingers closing around his, the warmth of his skin a sudden, sharp sensation.

Chapter 12: The Collective Arrives & The Riven Council

Keket

During that same cycle, the respite within the crystal city, however fraught with its own impossible revelations and dawning intimacy, was short-lived. I was in the small, functional space assigned to me, reviewing the data logs from our controlled synchronization experiment from Chapter 11, the hum of the Scarabite-7 spire and a constant presence felt deep in my bones. Sekem was nearby, running diagnostics on a portable console he'd brought from the Barque, his brow furrowed in concentration. Joric was stationed just outside the door, his presence a quiet, reassuring weight. Bastet was likely still downlinking data in the designated tech bay, trying to make sense of the alien energy signatures with Terran tools. The air was thick with the aftermath of shared cosmic glimpses and the unsettling hum beneath the city – a subtle resonance I now associated with the Path and the chilling idea of something ancient watching, first sensed.

Suddenly, a chime, sharp and insistent, resonated directly within my mind – a priority alert. Overriding the local network. Originating from the Celestial Barque. My comm panel flared crimson.

"Report, Joric," I subvocalized instantly, activating the secure comm link, my hand going to the interface point behind my ear. Sekem looked up sharply from his console, his usual calm cracking. Lieutenant Joric's voice was clipped, efficient, but undeniably laced with an undercurrent of urgency that pricked my nerves. Mirroring the sudden, sharp tension in the air.

"Captain, priority communique received from Sah Collective Command. Encrypted, urgent. Direct channel override. They're... they're hailing the planet, Captain." His voice was strained. Fear, raw and sudden, surged through his tone. My stomach tightened. A cold knot forming. Command rarely pinged with such immediacy. Bypassing standard protocols. Unless something significant. Something critical. Was unfolding.

"Patch it through, Lieutenant. Full encryption. Sekem, get a read on the source signature. Bastet, report to my location immediately, secure channel." Data streams flooded my neural interface. Bypassing Ma'at's polite synthesis for raw, coded information. Reports scrolled past my vision – supply chain analyses, colony stability projections, resource allocation charts. All grim. Increased pressure on the hyperlane network. Bottlenecks worsening faster than projected. Several developing colonies facing critical shortages – Cygnus X-1 Prime, the Kepler settlements, the outer rim outposts. The need for stable Phase-Channel conduits, the need for Scarabite-7, had escalated. From strategically vital to acutely critical. A galactic emergency. The subtext was clear. Stark. Demanding: Get it done, Captain. Yesterday.

"Source signature confirmed, Captain," Sekem reported, his voice tight. His eyes wide with alarm as he read his console. "It's a Collective dreadnought. Invictus class. Heavy armament. And... they're in high orbit. They didn't even send a scout." His stoic demeanor faltered, replaced by raw fear. "Captain, what is going on? Command doesn't deploy an Invictus unless it's a... a show of force. Or worse." The sheer power, the implication of a warship appearing without warning, slammed into me.

Joric, ever the security specialist, added, his voice low and tense from the doorway, "Proximity alarms on the Barque are screaming, Captain. They're running active scans, deep-penetration. Our shield harmonics are holding, but... this isn't a diplomatic approach. We need to know their intent." The weight of my mission, temporarily overshadowed by the sheer, world-altering weirdness of the Nexus Path and my impossible connection to Zephyr, slammed back into me with full force. Amplified by my crew's fear. My crew waited in orbit. Vulnerable. The Collective demanded results. And now, it seemed, they were here to take them. Entire settlements potentially depended on what lay beneath this planet's surface. And the key to it all seemed inextricably tied to the enigmatic, compelling warrior-leader who held this world's secrets, and who I had just... shared a moment of profound connection with. The jarring transition from the quiet intensity of reviewing Path data to the blaring alarm and my crew's panic was a physical shock. The stakes had just become terrifyingly real and immediate.

Zephyr

Zephyr stood before the Kryll High Council. The chamber, carved deep within the city's foundational crystal, hummed with ancient power and present tension. The air is thick with the weight of history and conflicting ideologies. Light refracted through intricate formations, casting shifting patterns on the stern, often fearful, faces of the Elders seated in a semi-circle before him. He maintained a facade of controlled stoicism, posture erect, hands clasped loosely behind his back, projecting the calm authority expected of the First Light lineage, the Protector. But beneath the surface, his own energy field thrummed with a mixture of apprehension, resolve, and the lingering, disorienting echo of Keket's starlight energy. The unsettling hum beneath the city, the one I now tied to the chaotic Path activation from Chapter 8 and potential ancient attention, felt amplified here, a constant low-frequency tremor against my control.

"...and so, the off-worlder, Keket, Captain of the vessel Celestial Barque, remains within our city," he concluded, his voice resonant and even, presenting the facts with deliberate neutrality. "She seeks Scarabite-7, a mineral vital to her people's travel between stars. More significantly, her arrival, her unique energy signature interacting with our own systems and the Heartstone, appears to have reawakened... aspects of the Nexus Path."

A murmur ran through the council. A ripple of fear. Unease. Elder Vorin, his face etched with the deep lines of centuries and suspicion, his bioluminescent patterns muted, leaned forward, his voice a dry, rasping sound that carried the weight of remembered trauma. "Reawakened? Zephyr, you speak of legends best left dormant! The Path brought ruin once! The Unraveling! This 'Great Mistake' cost us dearly, shattered our world, nearly extinguished our light! Are we to invite such chaos again, merely for an outsider's needs, for a power we sealed away in terror?" His fear was palpable, a current running through the chamber. Amplified by the nervous energy of other Elders. "Some of us warned against any interaction with off-worlders after the Unraveling, against seeking knowledge from the void. This proves our caution was justified!" His bioluminescence flared with overt fear and condemnation.

Another Elder, Lyra, known for her cautious pragmatism rather than outright fear, her bioluminescent patterns shifting with controlled anxiety, added, "An outsider whose technology interacts directly with our core systems? Who triggered uncontrolled energy surges upon arrival? Bringing her into the heart of our protected city... Zephyr, the risk is unprecedented. Some already whisper this decision challenges the wisdom of your leadership, that you are too... fascinated by this anomaly." Her words, though less overtly fearful than Vorin's, hinted at political maneuvering and a challenge to his authority, likely from factions who favored stricter isolation and distrusted his approach – the subtle divisions I had sensed now becoming verbalized dissent.

Zephyr met their gazes, one by one, acknowledging the fear and the political currents. He saw the ingrained distrust born from past trauma, the different interpretations of the Great Mistake – some seeing it as a consequence of the Path itself, others as a consequence of interacting with outsiders, others still as a failure of internal control. He held his ground, drawing on generations of resilience, on the conviction that ignorance was a greater threat than calculated risk. "The risk is acknowledged, Elders," he stated, his tone firm but respectful, unwavering. "Yet, the interaction has occurred. The Path has responded to her presence. Ignoring it, sending Captain Keket away without understanding the phenomenon she represents, without understanding why she resonates with Xylos in this way, could be equally dangerous. She may be a key, not just to the Path, but to preventing another Unraveling." He wouldn't mention the prophecy, the mate aspect – that was knowledge too volatile for this forum, too personal, too easily misinterpreted as manipulation or a grab for power.

"I have implemented enhanced monitoring protocols throughout the city and around the off-world vessel," he continued, outlining the strategic adjustments to the city's energy field monitoring and internal security patrols, measures already underway. "The Captain is contained, observed, but she is also collaborating. Her need for Scarabite-7 aligns, for now, with our need to understand this reawakened potential. Caution guides us, Elders, but ignorance will not serve us in the face of this... new reality." He projected decisive command, overriding their skepticism with sheer force of will, presenting his actions as necessary steps for the survival of Xylos.

Elder Vorin scoffed, his bioluminescence flaring with disapproval. "Collaboration with an outsider? While the echoes of the Unraveling still resonate in the Heartstone? This is folly, Zephyr! The Path should remain sealed! The knowledge buried! Our strength lies in our isolation, in the purity of our own light!" His words resonated with the hardline isolationist view, the ideology that would later coalesce into Faction Twelve, fearful of all external influence.

"Isolation did not prevent the Unraveling entirely, Elder Vorin," Zephyr countered, his voice holding a subtle edge, a reminder of the cost of that past catastrophe. "And the universe outside our shield has changed. Ignoring it will not make it disappear." He felt eyes on him from the chamber's entrance. Keket. She stood quietly, observing the proceedings, her expression carefully neutral, a study in Terran composure. Yet, he saw the intelligence in her green eyes, assessing the political currents, the weight of his responsibility, the different factions laid bare in the council's debate. For a fleeting moment, her focused intensity seemed a point of calm in the storm of the council's anxieties, a shared understanding that transcended the heated words. Then he caught himself. Focus, Zephyr. Her presence complicated everything, challenged his control in ways he was only beginning to understand. Why did the sight of her, even standing passively, send a disruptive current through his carefully maintained composure?

The council session concluded, leaving Zephyr drained but resolute. The pushback had been significant, fueled by fear of the past and suspicion of the outsider. He retreated not to his official chambers, but to a high balcony overlooking the city, a place where he often came to reconnect with Xylos's hum, to find a moment of peace amidst the turmoil. He needed to center himself. Lifting his hands, he began to shape the ambient light, coaxing it into complex, shifting crystalline forms that hovered and spun in the air before him – a focused skill, part meditation, part practice, a way to reconnect with the city's energy.

But his focus fractured. Images intruded: Keket's face in the council chamber, her perceptive green eyes; the memory of her hand in his, the shocking intimacy of the shared visions, the terrifying potential of the Path. Why can't I stop thinking about her? Her presence was a disruption, a variable he hadn't accounted for, a constant hum beneath his thoughts. He compared her directness, even her occasional bluntness, to the veiled language of his council, to the fear that masked their true intentions. She was... different. Not just alien, but possessing a clarity, a drive, that he found both unnerving and compelling. He forced the thoughts away, focusing on the light patterns, trying to reassert control. Liking her – the thought felt absurd, dangerous. She was an off-worlder, the potential catalyst for unknown powers, a complication to his rule, a risk to his people. The Great Mistake had taught them the price of uncontrolled interaction with external forces, the price of letting the wrong kind of light into their world. Attachment was a vulnerability he couldn't afford. His duty was to Xylos, to the Kryll. Full stop.

Yet... the memory of her loneliness, the sheer determination he'd felt in her vision of navigating the void, the hope she represented for something beyond isolation... it sparked something else. Not just fascination, but a reluctant stirring of... protectiveness? The thought of her facing the cold emptiness between stars, or facing the Collective's demands alone, or facing the fear of his own people... it settled uncomfortably in his chest. He mentally berated himself. Focus on the mission, the threat, not the traveler.

(Administrator Vorlann's POV - Unchanged from original)

Aboard the bridge of the Collective dreadnought Invictus, Administrator Vorlann permitted herself a grimace as the Kryll leader's defiant image vanished from the main screen. The feedback surge from their shield had sent minor Klaxons shrieking – an unexpected level of energy redirection.

"Report," she snapped, turning to her tactical officer, a pale man whose fingers flew across his console.

"Minimal damage, Administrator. Shield harmonics stabilized. But their shield technology... it resonates on frequencies we haven't encountered. Layered, adaptive".

Vorlann paced the command deck, the rhythmic click of her boots echoing faintly. Primitives clinging to protocol while sitting on the key to galactic dominance. The pressure from High Command – specifically from Admiral Sarkov's expansionist bloc – was immense. The whispers about the 'Nexus Path', initially dismissed as fringe science, had gained traction in the intelligence directorate. Control the Path, control all faster-than-light travel, bypass the congested hyperlanes entirely. An advantage Sarkov would use to reshape the Collective, sideline the dithering diplomats on Diaspora, and secure humanity's– his– absolute supremacy.

"They mentioned Keket by name," Vorlann mused aloud. "The Watcher pilot assigned to the initial Scarabite-7 survey. She's involved. Perhaps she is the key".

Failure was not an option. Sarkov didn't tolerate failure. She activated a secure channel. "Tactical, prepare targeted seismic probes. If they won't open the door, we'll knock it down. Let's see how their 'sovereignty' holds up when their world starts shaking".

Keket:

While the tense exchange continued in the council chamber, and the city's shields hummed under the distant pressure of the Invictus, my attention was drawn to the city beyond the lab's shielded viewports. Through the golden glow of the shield, I saw Kryll citizens moving with purpose, some faces set with determination, others pale with fear, their bioluminescent patterns muted or flickering with anxiety. I overheard hushed, urgent arguments nearby – factions forming, old fears resurfacing, the trauma of the Great Mistake and the fear of outsiders tearing at the city's unity. The arrival of outsiders, especially the Collective, was clearly divisive, a catalyst for internal conflict, exacerbating the subtle energy modulations and different energy signatures I'd sensed earlier.

A priority alert flashed on Zephyr's console, drawing his attention away from the main viewscreen. He listened intently, his expression darkening further with grim realization. "There was an energy surge near the Celestial Barque's docking cradle," he told me, his voice low, tight with concern. "Subtle, masked by the Collective's scan attempt. Could be environmental, could be..." He didn't finish, but the implication was clear: sabotage. An attack on my ship, on my crew. "The external sensors on your ship need verification. They might provide telemetry the Collective could exploit if they gain access, a backdoor into our systems."

He assigned two of his elite guard – tall, imposing Kryll clad in shimmering, articulated armor, their energy staffs humming with contained power. "Escort Keket to her vessel. Ensure its systems are secure. Verify external sensor integrity. Maximum vigilance. Report any hostile contact immediately."

The path to the Barque led through older, quieter sectors of the city, away from the central spire, where ancient Xylos flora intertwined with the Kryll architecture, creating a beautiful but potentially dangerous labyrinth. The air felt heavy, charged not just by the shield but by unseen eyes, by the tension of a city on edge. My senses, heightened by the calibration and the events of the past day – the intense Path glimpse, the unsettling echoes I now perceived – were on high alert. Picking up subtle shifts in energy, faint tremors in the stone beneath my feet that weren't tied to geological activity. These were the energy signatures of unseen Kryll moving through hidden passages, some pulsing with fear, others with a cold, directed aggression I now recognized from the dissenting voices in the council.

As we passed a shadowed archway overgrown with phosphorescent vines, movement flickered in the periphery of my vision. Blinding green energy bolts sizzled through the air, impacting the crystalline pathway near my feet with explosive force, sending shards skittering across the ground.

"Ambush!" one of the guards yelled, his voice sharp, shoving me hard behind a thick, root-like buttress as he activated his shimmering personal shield – just in time to absorb a direct hit that sent rippling shockwaves across its surface, the energy dissipating with a crackle. The other guard spun, energy staff flaring, not just deflecting but catching a bolt and redirecting it back towards the shadows with a fluid, deadly grace. Phosphorescent vines exploded where the redirected bolt struck, revealing fleeting shapes in the gloom. I saw the markings on their dark fatigues... The attackers were Kryll.

I recognized the markings on their dark fatigues... This wasn't the Collective. This was internal betrayal. A civil conflict is erupting around me. Turning Zephyr's own people into a threat. It was a gut punch. A cold reminder that the trust I was cautiously extending to Zephyr and his world was a dangerous gamble. Potentially fatal.

The fight was brutal and close-quarters in the narrow passage. The guards moved with fluid grace, their staffs humming, creating arcs of defensive energy and unleashing precise blasts of contained power. I drew my pulse pistol, firing quick, suppressive shots towards the muzzle flashes, providing covering fire, my training kicking in despite the shock of being attacked by Zephyr's own people. The air grew thick with the smell of ozone and superheated crystal. An attacker cried out, stumbling back from behind a cluster of glowing fungi, clutching their arm, hit by one of the guard's redirected blasts. But there were more than expected, melting out of the shadows. One guard grunted, staggering back, his shield flickering as an energy bolt overloaded it, scoring a burn across his shoulder pauldron. They were being driven back, forced towards a cliff edge where the city met a chasm filled with pulsating, toxic fungi clouds, a sheer drop into poisonous luminescence.

I fumbled for a tech grenade, my fingers slick with sweat, my mind racing for an option. A bolt sizzled past my head, impacting the rock beside me with a sharp crack. Cornered.

"Commander! We are engaged! Hostile Kryll forces! Sector Gamma-Niner! Ambush!" the uninjured guard relayed into his comm, even as he parried another blow, his shield straining.

Zephyr's voice, strained but sharp with immediate understanding, instantly crackled in my own earpiece, overriding Sekem's panicked attempts to reach me, his command cutting through the chaos. "Keket! Status! Are you secure? Guards, deploy pattern Delta! Reinforcements en route – hold for thirty seconds!" His tactical orders cut through chaos. Precise and decisive. I risked a glance over the edge – a dizzying drop into swirling, poisonous luminescence, not an option for retreat. Seeing an opportunity, a weakness in the attackers' formation near the unstable edge, I hurled my grenade not at them directly, but bounced it off the archway wall to land precisely amongst the attackers near the unstable rock formation. The explosion wasn't lethal, but it sent shards of rock and crystal flying, creating a momentary diversion, a shockwave that staggered them. It was just enough. More Kryll guards, alerted by Zephyr, rappelled down from higher levels, converging on the attackers from above and behind. The firefight intensified briefly, then subsided as the ambushers, realizing they were outnumbered and outmaneuvered, melted back into the shadows, disappearing into the labyrinthine passages they knew so well.

Breathless, uniform torn, the sting of ozone sharp in my nostrils, Keket was helped back from the precipice by the injured guard, his arm bleeding but his resolve firm. I met Zephyr's intense gaze moments later as he arrived with the main reinforcement squad, his relief warring visibly with cold fury directed at the unseen enemy within his own people, at the betrayal that had just unfolded.

Just then, Just then, Administrator Vorlann's voice cut through the city-wide comms again, colder and more imperious than before, a chilling echo of the Collective's reach. The timing wasn't a coincidence; the Collective's deep scans had likely detected the energy spikes from the internal sabotage, revealing a vulnerability at the worst possible moment. "Commander Zephyr. Our sensors detected localized weapons fire within your settlement. Report immediately. This... internal instability... strengthens the Collective's mandate to intervene for regional security. It suggests your leadership is... compromised." The ambush, already terrifying, had just handed the enemy the perfect justification to escalate.

"Commander Zephyr. Our sensors detected localized weapons fire within your settlement. Report immediately. This... internal instability... strengthens the Collective's mandate to intervene for regional security. It suggests your leadership is... compromised." Zephyr looked from me, shaken but alive, to the viewscreen displaying the implacable Collective ship hanging above, a brutalist threat in the sky, then back towards the shadowed archways where his own people had tried to kill me, where the internal conflict festered. He was trapped – an aggressor fleet above, betrayal festering within his own city, and the woman who represented both unprecedented hope and catastrophic risk standing right beside him, a target for both external and internal enemies. The boundaries weren't just being tested anymore; they were crumbling, and the choices ahead would be harder than anything either of us had ever faced.

Chapter 13: Testing the Boundaries

The 'night' cycle had fallen, and the ambient, bioluminescent glow of Xylos's flora painted the laboratory in shifting patterns of emerald and sapphire. The 'night' cycle had fallen, a period of relative quiet on the vibrant world, yet inside the repurposed research outpost, the air hummed with a tension that resonated deeper than the thrum of the localized energy field dampeners. The lingering echoes of their initial, almost accidental brush with the Nexus Path, the raw, untamed potential they'd glimpsed, the chilling sense of having alerted something ancient – now had to be channeled, understood, and controlled. It felt like stepping onto the edge of an abyss, tethered only by a fragile hypothesis and a terrifying, undeniable connection.

Zephyr stood before the central console, the intricate patterns on his arms shimmering faintly, a visual echo of the spire's own internal light. His usual calm was overlaid with a rigid formality I hadn't seen before. It was the posture of command, yes, demanding control. But beneath it, I sensed the coiled spring of apprehension. The Great Mistake, the oft-alluded-to Kryll catastrophe tied to uncontrolled energetic exploration, was no mere historical footnote for him; it was ingrained caution, a genetic memory etched into his very being. It felt less like history and more like a raw, open wound his people barely survived. This caution warred visibly with the undeniable magnetic pull of the Path, the profound implications of what it represented, and the unexpected synergy he felt with me, the off-worlder who somehow resonated with Xylos's deepest secrets.

"Power conduits stable," I reported, my voice steady despite the prickle of anticipation crawling up my spine. The humming crystals of the apparatus felt charged, the air thick with latent energy. "Resonance chamber cycling at baseline. Field emitters... nominal."

"Initiate sequence protocols," Zephyr ordered, his voice leaving no room for debate. Crisp. Precise. "Minimal effective yield. Safety overrides engaged at threshold delta-seven. Monitor bio-signatures constantly. Any deviation beyond predicted parameters, immediate shutdown." His directives were a physical manifestation of his caution – drawing lines in the energetic sand that

I, in my purely scientific enthusiasm, might have otherwise crossed too quickly. He understood intimately the cost of failure.

I nodded, fingers flying across my console. The Weaving Crystals at the heart of our apparatus pulsed brighter, a low thrum intensifying. The air grew thick, charged. The low, unsettling hum I'd sensed in the city since the uncontrolled Path activation seemed to deepen here, vibrating through the floor, a subtle discord beneath the apparatus' rising energy. Then, it hit them. Not a sound. Not a light show. An immersion.

Fractured images, chaotic sensations flooded my mind: the impossible geometry of folded space, the whisper of alien thoughts like dry leaves skittering across consciousness, the chilling vastness between stars compressed into a single, terrifying point. And interwoven with the cosmic glimpses, brief, horrifying flashes – a scream swallowed by silence, a shadow that moved with impossible speed, the feeling of being watched by something vast and indifferent. Fleeting. Disturbing. Subtle signs that the Path held more than just potential; it held ancient, unsettling inhabitants or memories. Glimpses into the Path. More intense than our preliminary exposure, raw and overwhelming. And interwoven with the cosmic glimpses, brief, horrifying flashes – a scream swallowed by silence, a shadow that moved with impossible speed, the feeling of being watched by something vast and indifferent. Fleeting. Disturbing. Subtle signs that the Path held more than just potential; it held ancient, unsettling inhabitants or memories. I gasped, gripping the edge of my console, anchoring myself against the psychic tide.

The connection snapped off as abruptly as it began, triggered by Zephyr's swift override. Silence rushed back in, heavy and profound. The only sound, the residual hum of the crystals and my own ragged breathing. I blinked, disorientation making the lab lights seem too bright. The lingering scent of ozone and charged energy prickled my nostrils. I looked at Zephyr. He stood ramrod straight, his expression unreadable, a mask of perfect composure. But as he turned from the main controls, his hand brushed against a data slate, and I saw it – a faint, almost imperceptible tremor before he consciously stilled it. A moment later, when his gaze met hers, the cool assessment was there, but behind it, for a fleeting second, was a haunted quality, a shadow that spoke of horrors witnessed. He saw me watching, and saw the question in my eyes.

He didn't address the tremor directly but gestured towards a thin, silvery scar tracing a line from his temple partially into his scaled hairline. "Caution is not cowardice, Keket," he said, his voice quiet but firm. "It is wisdom bought with pain. Some energies are not meant to be trifled lightly." He offered no further explanation, the scar serving as a tangible symbol of past crises, proof of the hard-won capability behind his insistence on control. The moment passed. The mask firmly back in place.

The hours between experiments stretched, marked by the soft hum of monitoring equipment and the rhythmic pulse of Xylos's nocturnal life outside. The intensity of the tests left a residual charge in the air, a shared vulnerability that chipped away at their professional distance. We fell into a pattern – analyzing data, recalibrating, and talking.

Zephyr, perhaps sensing my need for grounding after the disorienting glimpses into the Path, began to share carefully curated fragments about Xylos. He spoke of its unique bio-energetic field, how the planet itself seemed to possess a form of slow, geological consciousness, how the Kryll believed their own evolution was intrinsically tied to harmonizing with these planetary rhythms. He described the subtle energy flows the Weaving Crystals harnessed, knowledge withheld from most off-world inquiries, offered now as a cautious gesture of trust, an unexpected point of shared scientific interest.

I, in turn, found myself describing the stars not as abstract destinations, but as places I had been. I spoke of the cold, sterile beauty of orbital stations, the chaotic energy of Earth cities, the relentless drive of corporate expansion that had pushed humanity outward. I described the sensory overload, the constant barrage of information, the feeling of being perpetually adrift in a sea of noise and ambition, the very "ground static" that had made me restless, driving me to seek something more, something represented by the Watcher legacy Jax seemed to both covet and misunderstand.

Zephyr listened intently, his head tilted, his multifaceted eyes seeming to absorb not just my words but the emotions beneath them. When I finished describing a particularly soulless corporate gathering on Mars, he was quiet for a long moment. "Your people," he began, his voice soft, thoughtful, choosing his words with deliberate care, "their minds seem so loud. Constantly filled with noise, focused outward on fleeting things – status, possessions, conflicts."

He wasn't judging, I realized, but observing, analyzing from a fundamentally different perspective.

"True connection, deep evolution," he continued, his gaze distant, as if peering into cosmic principles, "it often requires stillness. An ability to quiet the internal chatter, to listen – to the self, to the world, to the energies between. Many advanced paths require that inner quiet. Without it, awareness remains... superficial. Unable to perceive the deeper currents, like those we touch through the Path." He looked back at me then, a considering light in his eyes. "Perhaps your lineage," he mused, "your heightened senses... they allow you to perceive frequencies others of your kind miss. Cut some of that noise. It might be why you resonate with the Path, why we can attempt this." The implication hung in the air – my difference was not just a quirk, but potentially a key. His words created a subtle tension, a prompt for me to defend my species, yet also a profound acknowledgment of my unique place in this endeavor.

Simultaneously, beneath his philosophical observations, I sensed another current. When I spoke of the starship drives, the feeling of acceleration, the view of nebulae through a viewport, a flicker of something akin to longing crossed Zephyr's features. "To see another star," he murmured once, almost to himself, "to feel the pull of a different gravity... it is a concept that Kryll understands theoretically, but few have experienced." A conflict surfaced briefly – the unwavering dedication to his duty, his world, his people, brushing against a deep, perhaps suppressed, desire for the vast unknown she represented.

Later, after another experiment pushed the boundaries further than intended, the danger became starkly real. A feedback loop ignited within the resonance chamber. Alarms shrieked. Blue energy arced violently, striking a secondary console and sending sparks showering down. I yelped, jerking back as a wave of heat washed over my arm, leaving a faint red mark. Zephyr slammed his hand down on the emergency containment field, the shimmering barrier snapping into place just as a larger surge threatened to overload the primary systems. The lab plunged into emergency lighting, the silence deafening after the cacophony. The near-miss left us both shaken, the acrid smell of ozone sharp in the air. The chaotic visions accompanying the surge had been worse this time – images of collapsing realities, whispers turning into screams. Psychological shrapnel.

"That was too close," Zephyr grated, his voice tight with controlled fury and fear as he checked the scorched console. The smell of burnt circuitry filled the air, mingling with the ozone. "But we learned more!" I countered, adrenaline still singing in my veins, overriding the sting on my arm. The memory of collapsing realities made my voice tight. The acrid smell of ozone stinging my nostrils. The sting on my arm pulsed, a physical reminder of how real, how dangerous, this was. "But this is it, Zephyr! This is the edge of the unknown I left everything to find! This isn't optimizing cargo routes or analyzing sterile scans – this is a real discovery! We can't stop just because it's dangerous. We analyze the spike, adjust the frequency, and try again. That's how we move forward! That's why I'm here! That's what the Watcher legacy is for – to push boundaries, to see what others can't, not just feed a machine!" The "ground static" felt a million light-years away. The pull of this terrifying frontier was absolute, overriding caution, overriding fear, overriding the residual tremor in her hands. It was a clash of worlds, of philosophies, and the raw energy of their disagreement crackled between them, potent as the arcing blue light that had just nearly consumed the lab.

The Great Mistake loomed large in his voice. "We proceed with the caution I dictated, or we do not proceed at all!" The argument hung between them, raw and unresolved. My scientific drive, my ingrained human push to explore and conquer, slammed directly against his deep-seated, historically justified caution. The path ahead wasn't just technically challenging; it was tearing at the fragile trust we were building.

Hours later, the emergency lights still cast long shadows. The damage was contained, the systems slowly being brought back online, but the emotional fallout lingered. Exhaustion warred with residual adrenaline. We sat in silence for a long time, the weight of the day pressing down. I finally looked up, meeting Zephyr's gaze across the dimly lit space. The earlier anger had faded, replaced by a weariness that mirrored my own, but also something else – an intensity heightened by the danger we had shared. The fear, the near-miss, the clash of wills – it had stripped away layers of reserve.

He rose and came to her, stopping just inches away. The air crackled, not with failing energy fields, but with a different kind of potential. He reached out, his scaled fingers gently brushing the reddened skin on my arm where the energy surge had kissed me. His touch was surprisingly warm.

"Are you harmed?" he asked, his voice low, rough.

"No," I whispered, my breath catching. "Just... startled."

His eyes searched for mines, the multifaceted depths reflecting the dim light. The control he usually maintained so fiercely seemed to fracture. The memory of the chaotic visions, the brush with uncontrolled power, the fear of loss – it all converged with the undeniable pull between us. A desperate need for grounding in the face of the terrifying unknown we were exploring. Danger, a voice screamed, echoing ancient warnings. Consequences. But the need, raw and overwhelming, drowned out the fear.

With a sound that was almost a growl, Zephyr closed the remaining distance. His hand slid from my arm to cup the back of my neck, pulling me closer. There was no hesitation now, no carefully measured approach. His mouth claimed mine in a kiss that was fierce, almost desperate. It tasted of the day's fear, the adrenaline, but underneath was a deep, possessive need for connection, a grounding in the face of the terrifying unknown they were exploring. It wasn't gentle; it was assertive, demanding, a raw expression of the vulnerability the Path – and their proximity – had exposed within him. He held me tightly, as if anchoring himself not just to her, but to the present moment, away from the ghosts of the past and the terrifying potential of the future. The kiss deepened, a flare of heat in the cool, damaged lab, a testament to boundaries tested, and irrevocably, shatteringly, crossed. The kiss wasn't an end, but an ignition. Zephyr's lips moved against mines, demanding and hungry, the earlier fear transmuting into raw, undeniable need. I responded with equal fervor, my hands coming up to grip his shoulders, anchoring herself in the storm. I could taste the faint metallic tang of adrenaline from his sweat, mixed with something uniquely Zephyr, earthy and unfamiliar, a flavor as alien and intoxicating as the world outside. His hand tightened at my nape, fingers tangling in my hair, while his other arm circled my waist, crushing me against him. I could feel the surprising heat radiating from him, far warmer than she'd expected, and the hard lines of his cock pressing against her. Beneath the thin fabric of her uniform, she could discern the subtle give of muscle and, intriguing me even through the haze of desire, the underlying pattern of smooth, fine scales covering his torso – not rough or reptilian, but like polished river stones, cool initially but rapidly warming to his internal heat leading to his penis. The sound of our harsh breathing filled the small space, punctuated by soft gasps. The background hum of the emergency systems seemed to fade into irrelevance. I could almost hear the frantic thrumming of my own heart, feeling it echoed by the powerful beat I could sense through Zephyr's chest against mine. He broke the kiss only to trail fire along her jawline, his lips surprisingly soft against her skin, sending shivers down my spine despite the warmth flushing through her. He straightened up, pulling away slightly, though his eyes never left hers. The fierce heat in his gaze flickered, replaced by something akin to shock, then dawning realization – perhaps horror at his own loss of control. The careful walls, breached by danger and desire, began to reconstruct themselves with visible effort. He took a ragged breath, the sound harsh in the sudden quiet. The shadow of the Great Mistake, of consequences born from impulsive action, seemed to fall over him once more. He didn't speak, but I could see the internal battle raging within him. The boundary hadn't just been tested; it had nearly been obliterated.

Chapter 14: The Collective Arrives & The Ambush in the Labyrinth

Keket

With the dawn of the next cycle, the silence in the lab following Zephyr's abrupt withdrawal was thick with unspoken words and unresolved tension. The heat of the moment lingered, tangible and electric, a raw current in the air, even as a chasm of awkwardness opened between us. I could still feel the ghost of his touch, the imprint of his lips, the startling heat of his scaled skin against mine. He stood rigidly across the room, his back half-turned, the turmoil visible in the tight line of his shoulders, a battle raging within him that mirrored the one in my own mind. What now? Where did we go from—

WHOOP. WHOOP. WHOOP.

The jarring shriek of city-wide alarms shattered the fragile quiet. A sudden, piercing sound that ripped through the silence like a physical blow. Emergency lights, already casting long shadows in the lab, now pulsed an urgent, frantic crimson, bathing the room in a pulsing, dangerous glow. The subtle, unsettling hum beneath the city, the one I now associated with the Path and the chilling idea of something ancient watching since Chapter 9 and 10, seemed to spike, discordant and frantic.

Zephyr spun around, the internal conflict instantly vaporizing, replaced by the hard mask of command I had seen earlier, now amplified tenfold by the sudden, external threat. His eyes, sharp and focused, locked onto the main viewscreen as it flickered to life, displaying the upper atmosphere of Xylos, a view that stole my breath. Hanging there, stark and immense against the swirling blues and greens of the daytime sky, was a ship utterly alien to Xylos's organic aesthetic, a brutalist intrusion into this living world. It wasn't merely large; it was a kilometer-long wedge of gunmetal grey armor plating, a brutalist monument to function over form – the unmistakable, terrifying signature of a Sah Collective dreadnought, the *Invictus*. It bristled with turrets, sensor arrays, and the ominous, gaping apertures of heavy energy cannons. Radiating cold efficiency and overwhelming power. A stark, chilling contrast to the subtle energies of the living city below. Smaller fighter craft moved in disciplined, predatory patrols around its perimeter, their engines leaving faint ion trails against the alien sky, like vultures circling. It was the unmistakable signature of the Interstellar Collective, and they were here. The sheer, overwhelming scale of it was a punch to the gut, a brutal reminder of the sterile, expansionist force I had tried to escape, now looming over the fragile, vibrant world below.

"They are here," Zephyr breathed, the words tight with grim finality, a recognition of the inevitable confrontation. He was already moving, barking orders in rapid, sibilant Kryll into his comm unit, his voice sharp and decisive. Around the city, I heard the deep thrum of power intensifying as massive energy conduits rerouted, the very structure of the city responding to his command. Outside the lab viewport, a subtle shimmer resolved into a vast, dome-like energy shield snapping into place over the Kryll settlement, bathing everything in a faint golden light, a visible manifestation of Xylos's defenses. Pre-planned defensive measures, executed with chilling speed and efficiency. His strategic acumen was formidable. Undeniable.

He gestured me towards a tactical display illuminating a nearby wall, bringing up schematics and energy readings. "The Collective does not make social calls unannounced, Captain," he stated, his voice devoid of the warmth, the vulnerability, from moments before. He was Kryll Commander Zephyr now, Protector of Xylos, his focus solely on the external threat. "Their arrival signals intent, likely aggressive, concerning you and the Nexus Path technology they have somehow detected." He tapped commands, bringing up potential ship configurations and known Collective protocols, analyzing their likely strategy. "We must assume they know something. We need a unified strategy, and we need it now."

His eyes met hers, intense and assessing, demanding my professional input, my Terran perspective on the Collective's methods. "I suggest we immediately initiate broad-spectrum communication jamming, targeting their known internal fleet frequencies. Disrupt their coordination before negotiations even begin, before they can fully assess our capabilities or coordinate an attack."

I frowned, my mind racing through Collective protocols and diplomatic norms. "Isn't that... overly provocative? A potential first strike? It could escalate the situation immediately."

Zephyr's expression hardened further, his jaw set with grim determination. "They drop an *Invictus* class dreadnought into orbit uninvited above a sovereign world, running deep scans? They are invaders until proven otherwise,

Captain. Proactive defense is not provocation; it is survival. It is the lesson etched into our history." His decisiveness was absolute, bordering on ruthless – a moral ambiguity I found unsettling in its cold logic, yet strategically sound in our precarious position. He then added, his gaze unwavering, his voice dropping slightly but losing none of its steel, "And let this be understood clearly: When they demand you, the answer is no. You discovered the Path here, Keket. You are currently engaged in research vital to Xylos. You are under Kryll protection." The assertiveness was sharp, territorial, leaving no room for argument, a declaration of ownership that sent an unexpected tremor through me, a complex mix of reassurance at his protection and alarm at the possessiveness underlying the declaration.

My personal comm pinged again, sharp and insistent, cutting through the tense air of the command hub. It was Sekem, his voice tight with barely suppressed panic, amplified by the comm's filter. "Acknowledged, Captain, that ship – it's Collective registry! An Invictus! What in the stars is going on? Our proximity alarms are screaming! We're getting bombarded with active scans! We need to lift off, get clear, Captain! We're sitting ducks up here!" His voice cracked with fear, underscoring the sheer, overwhelming power of the dreadnought and the terrifying vulnerability of our position.

"Hold position, Sekem," I ordered immediately, trying to project a calm I didn't feel, my voice steady despite the frantic beat of my heart. "Do not transmit anything further. Maintain strict radio silence unless absolutely necessary. We are... addressing the situation down here. Stay alert. Acknowledge."

"Acknowledged, Captain," Sekem replied, the panic still evident in his voice, but obedience ingrained. "Staying dark. Sekem out." The call highlighted the friction within my own small crew – their fear was justified, their instinct to flee a massive Collective warship was sound. My closeness to Zephyr, this alien leader making unilateral declarations of protection, was undoubtedly straining their trust, leaving them vulnerable and confused in orbit, cut off from familiar Collective channels, adding another layer to their apprehension about the deepening galactic crisis they only dimly perceived.

Bastet's voice crackled through next, sharp and anxious. "Captain, my sensors are picking up massive energy fluctuations from the planet! And the Collective ship is... it's attempting a forced scan! They're hitting the shield with everything they have! What do we do?" Her engineering brain, trained in predictable physics, was clearly struggling to process the immense, unfamiliar energy being unleashed.

"Bastet, monitor shield harmonics, log all energy signatures," I instructed, trying to keep my voice level. "Joric, keep your team on high alert, internal and external threats. We are now protected by planets. I'll update you when I can. Keket out."

A high-pitched whine emanated from the city's shield generators, a sound felt deep in my bones, a rising shriek of stressed energy. The shield was working, but it was straining. "Commander!" a Kryll technician reported urgently, his voice strained, eyes wide with an alarm fixed on his console. "Aggressive energy surge detected! The Collective vessel is attempting a forced deep-penetration scan! They're bypassing standard protocols!"

A blinding lance of focused energy erupted from the *Invictus*, visible even through the shield's golden glow, striking the invisible shield directly above the spire with terrifying force. The air screamed as the beam impacted, the golden dome flaring with incandescent intensity, pushing back against the invasive energy. The ground beneath my feet vibrate violently. The crystalline walls around us groaned under the strain, the very structure of the city protesting the assault. It wasn't just a scan; it was a battering ram made of pure power, designed to shatter defenses through sheer force, to break the planet's will.

"Reinforce shield harmonics! Divert all available power to the primary shield emitters!" Zephyr commanded, his voice a whip-crack of authority, his gaze fixed on the tactical display showing the shield's integrity dropping in the impacted sector. The golden dome outside flared visibly brighter, pushing back against the Collective's assault, and a low groan echoed through the structure as the shield repelled the intrusive scan, the energy rippling outwards. The Collective ship seemed to shimmer for a moment on the viewscreen, its systems likely reeling from the feedback of hitting the Kryll shield with such force. Vorlann's hologram, still active on a secondary display, flickered, her expression tightening with anger and frustration. The standoff had escalated beyond mere words; the Collective had fired the first shot, a clear act of aggression.

While the tense exchange continued, and the city's shields hummed under the distant pressure of the *Invictus*, my attention was drawn to the city beyond the lab's shielded viewports. Through the golden glow of the shield, I saw

Kryll citizens moving with purpose, some faces set with determination, others pale with fear, their bioluminescent patterns muted or flickering with anxiety. I overheard hushed, urgent arguments nearby – factions forming, old fears resurfacing, the trauma of the Great Mistake and the fear of outsiders tearing at the city's unity. The arrival of outsiders, especially the Collective, was clearly divisive, a catalyst for internal conflict, exacerbating the subtle energy modulations and different energy signatures I'd sensed earlier in the Kryll guards.

A priority alert flashed on Zephyr's console, drawing his attention away from the main viewscreen. He listened intently, his expression darkening further with grim realization. "There was an energy surge near the Celestial Barque's docking cradle," he told me, his voice low, tight with concern. "Subtle, masked by the Collective's scan attempt. Could be environmental, could be..." He didn't finish, but the implication was clear: sabotage. An attack on my ship, on my crew. The timing wasn't a coincidence; the chaos and stress on the city's systems caused by the Collective's aggressive scanning had provided cover, or perhaps a signal, for internal actors to strike. "The external sensors on your ship need verification. They might provide telemetry the Collective could exploit if they gain access, a backdoor into our systems."

He assigned two of his elite guard – tall, imposing Kryll clad in shimmering, articulated armor, their energy staffs humming with contained power. "Escort Keket to her vessel. Ensure its systems are secure. Verify external sensor integrity. Maximum vigilance. Report any hostile contact immediately."

The path to the Barque led through older, quieter sectors of the city, away from the central spire, where ancient Xylos flora intertwined with the Kryll architecture, creating a beautiful but potentially dangerous labyrinth. The air felt heavy, charged not just by the shield but by unseen eyes, by the tension of a city on edge. My senses, heightened by the calibration and the events of the past day – the intense Path glimpse, the unsettling echoes I now perceived, the subtle hum of the city's unease – were on high alert. Picking up subtle shifts in energy, faint tremors in the stone beneath my feet that weren't tied to geological activity. These were the energy signatures of unseen Kryll moving through hidden passages, some pulsing with fear, others with a cold, directed aggression I now recognized from the dissenting voices in the council.

As we passed a shadowed archway overgrown with phosphorescent vines, movement flickered in the periphery of my vision. Blinding green energy bolts sizzled through the air, impacting the crystalline pathway near Keket's feet with explosive force, sending razor-sharp shards skittering across the ground. "Ambush!" one of Zephyr's elite guards roared, his voice sharp, shoving Keket hard behind a thick, root-like buttress. His shimmering personal shield flared just in time to absorb a direct hit, rippling shockwaves across its surface before dissipating with a crackle of overloaded energy. The other guard, a blur of controlled Kryll fury, spun, his energy staff flaring. He didn't just deflect the next bolt; he caught it, the alien energy twisting in his grip before he redirected it back towards the shadows with fluid, deadly grace. Phosphorescent vines vaporized where the redirected bolt struck, revealing fleeting shapes in the gloom. Kryll. Attackers in dark fatigues, their movements swift and brutal. Faction Twelve. Internal betrayal. A cold knot of distrust tightened in Keket's gut, a sickening realization that the threat was woven into the very fabric of Zephyr's society.

The fight was brutal and close-quarters in the narrow passage, a desperate ballet of energy weapons and shattering crystal. Zephyr's guards moved with lethal efficiency, their humming staffs creating arcs of defensive energy, unleashing precise, devastating blasts of contained power. Keket drew her pulse pistol, the familiar weight a small comfort, firing quick, suppressive shots towards the muzzle flashes, providing covering fire despite the shock of being attacked by Zephyr's own people. The air grew thick with the acrid smell of ozone and superheated crystal. An attacker cried out, stumbling back from behind a cluster of glowing fungi, clutching a cauterized arm, hit by a guard's redirected blast. But more melted out of the shadows than expected, their numbers swelling the narrow passage. One guard grunted, staggering back, his shield flickering wildly as an energy bolt overloaded it, scoring a deep burn across his shoulder pauldron. They were being driven back, forced towards the chasm's edge, a sheer drop into pulsating, toxic fungi clouds, poisonous luminescence swirling in the depths below. Cornered, exposed, a terrifying fall awaited if their line broke.

"Commander! We are engaged! Hostile Kryll forces! Sector Gamma-Niner! Ambush!" the uninjured guard relayed into his comm, even as he parried another blow, his shield straining against a renewed barrage.

Zephyr's voice, strained but sharp with immediate understanding, instantly crackled in Keket's own earpiece, overriding Sekem's panicked attempts to reach me, his command cutting through the chaos. "Keket! Status! Are you secure? Guards, deploy pattern Delta! Reinforcements en route – hold for thirty seconds!" His tactical orders cut through chaos. Precise and decisive.

Zephyr:

The moment the alert for Keket's ambush hit his comm, a cold, primal fury had eclipsed all tactical considerations. His guards, pattern Delta, reinforcements – these were just words. The reality was a single, burning imperative: *Keket*. Her safety. The thought of those Faction Twelve traitors laying a hand on her, the woman who carried starlight in her eyes and challenged his soul, ignited a possessiveness so fierce it bordered on the savage. Every order he barked was underpinned by that singular, desperate focus.

Keket risked a glance over the edge – a dizzying drop into swirling, poisonous luminescence. No retreat. Seeing an opportunity, a weakness in the attackers' formation near the unstable edge, Keket fumbled for a tech grenade, her fingers slick with sweat, her mind racing for an option. A bolt sizzled past her head, impacting the rock beside her with a sharp crack. She hurled the grenade not at them directly, but bounced it off the archway wall to land precisely among the attackers near the unstable rock formation on the precipice. The explosion wasn't lethal, but it sent shards of rock and crystal flying, creating a momentary diversion, a shockwave that staggered them, pushing some precariously close to the edge. It was just enough.

Keket:

More Kryll guards, alerted by Zephyr, rappelled down from higher levels, converging on the attackers from above and behind, their energy staffs spitting retaliatory fire. The firefight intensified briefly, a desperate, lethal struggle in the narrow passage, then subsided as the ambushers, realizing they were outnumbered and outmaneuvered, melted back into the shadows, disappearing into the labyrinthine passages they knew so well, leaving behind only the acrid smell of ozone and the chilling knowledge of their betrayal.

Breathless, uniform torn, the sting of ozone sharp in her nostrils, Keket was helped back from the precipice by the injured guard, his arm bleeding but his resolve firm. The other guard stood sentinel, scanning the shadows, his energy staff still humming, ready. Keket met Zephyr's intense gaze moments later as he arrived with the main reinforcement squad, his relief warring visibly with cold fury directed at the unseen enemy within his own people, at the betrayal that had just unfolded. Just then, Administrator Vorlann's voice cut through the city-wide comms again, colder and more imperious than before, a chilling echo of the Collective's reach. The timing wasn't a coincidence; the Collective's deep scans, stressing the city's systems, had likely detected the energy spikes from the internal sabotage, revealing a vulnerability at the worst possible moment. "Commander Zephyr. Our sensors detected localized weapons fire within your settlement. Report immediately. This... internal instability... strengthens the Collective's mandate to intervene for regional security. It suggests your leadership is... compromised." The ambush, already terrifying, had just handed the enemy the perfect justification to escalate.

Zephyr looked from me, shaken but alive, to the viewscreen displaying the implacable Collective ship hanging above, a brutalist threat in the sky, then back towards the shadowed archways where his own people had tried to kill me, where the internal conflict festered. He was trapped – an aggressor fleet above, betrayal festering within his own city, and the woman who represented both unprecedented hope and catastrophic risk standing right beside him, a target for both external and internal enemies. The boundaries weren't just being tested anymore; they were crumbling, and the choices ahead would be harder than anything either of us had ever faced.

Chapter 15: Secrets of Scarabite-7, Shared Burden

Keket

Following the ambush, the acrid tang of discharged energy weaponry still hung faintly in the air as Zephyr and I returned to the relative sanctuary of the central command hub. The echoes of the ambush – the spitting crackle of energy bolts, the grunt of the injured guard staggering back, the sheer, dizzying drop into the chasm filled with pulsating, toxic fungi clouds I'd narrowly avoided – played behind my eyes like a broken holovid loop. It wasn't just the physical danger that rattled me; it was the betrayal. Zephyr's own people, turning on his guard, on me. A knot of cold distrust tightened in my gut. How could I navigate this place, rely on his protection, when the threat was woven into the very fabric of his society? The subtle energy modulations of unseen Kryll moving through hidden passages, first sensed, now felt explicitly menacing, tied to a willingness for violence.

Above us, silent and menacing, the Collective ship maintained its vigil, a brutalist shadow against the shielded sky. Administrator Vorlann's chilling message about 'internal instability' resonated, turning the Kryll's own dissent, the fear and anger of Faction Twelve, into a weapon the Collective could wield against them, and against me. The immediate threat of the Collective, amplified by the near-death experience of the ambush, made the air thick with tension.

The hours bled into the deep Xylos night cycle, but there was no rest, only a relentless, high-stakes tension. Zephyr moved with quiet, contained intensity, a different kind of energy than the raw power he'd shown earlier, coordinating security sweeps through the city's ancient, twisting passages and analyzing the fragmented data recovered from the ambush site. I watched him from the periphery of the command hub, the stark contrast between the ruthless commander making split-second tactical choices and the man whose touch had ignited something impossible in the lab only hours before, a jarring counterpoint in my mind. He moved between holographic displays with fluid, decisive movements, his knowledge of the city's intricate layout – its hidden passages, forgotten levels, and potential ambush points – proving innate, a part of his very being.

"Focus sensor sweeps on the Old Aquifer access tunnels below Sector Gamma-Niner," he instructed his security chief, his voice low but carrying absolute authority, cutting through the low hum of the command center. "Faction Twelve has historically utilized subterranean routes during periods of unrest. Seal all known exits." His fingers danced across a console, highlighting structural weaknesses and surveillance blind spots with chilling precision. Proven capability, honed over years of safeguarding his isolated world, a world now under siege from within and without.

As if on cue, a proximity alert shrieked through the command hub, a jarring sound that cut through the tense quiet, followed instantly by the shudder of a distant explosion echoing through the spire structure, a physical blow felt even here. Zephyr spun towards the tactical display as damage reports flooded in, painting sections of the holographic city red. "Report!" he barked, his voice tight with controlled urgency.

"Explosion near shield relay 4-Beta!" a strained voice crackled over the comm, laced with fear. "Heavy damage to the relay housing and primary power conduit! Attempted sabotage – they used shaped plasma charges! Shield integrity in that sector is dropping fast!"

Zephyr's response was immediate, cold, decisive. "Divert auxiliary power! Seal the sector grid – containment fields active! Deploy capture drones and Alpha squad, lethal force authorized if suspects resist capture. That relay must be stabilized now!" He paused, his jaw tight, then added grimly, the words landing like cold stones, "Damage to the adjacent nutrient conduit is acceptable if unavoidable to secure the saboteurs quickly. Minimum exposure time for personnel." I overheard the order, the calculated acceptance of collateral damage sending a chill down my spine. This wasn't just clinical strategy; it was the harsh reality of leadership under siege, where lives became variables in an impossible equation. Zephyr caught my eye across the command hub, his expression unreadable for a moment before he turned back to the tactical display, the weight of his decision settling visibly upon his shoulders, a burden he carried alone, yet one I felt the edge of.

Unable to settle, my mind a chaotic loop of the day's events – the terrifying closeness of the ambush, the constant pressure of the Collective above, the unsettling echo of Zephyr's kiss, the knowledge of my crew alone in orbit – I retreated to the small, spartan quarters assigned to me earlier. Sleep was impossible. How could I reconcile the capable Captain my crew needed, the woman navigating galactic threats, with the one whose hands still trembled, whose mind reeled from the violation of forced intimacy, whose body remembered an alien touch with confusing intensity? My personal vulnerability felt like a dangerous flaw in this high-stakes environment. The subtle, unsettling hum beneath the city, a resonance tied to the Path and the idea of something ancient watching since Chapter 9 and 10, felt louder here in the quiet, vibrating through the very crystal of the walls.

Driven by a desperate need for answers – or perhaps just distraction from the turmoil in my mind, from the unsettling echo of his touch – I returned to the now-quiet lab area, drawn back to the Nexus Path data. The air still held the faint, acrid smell of ozone from the earlier feedback loop. Ignoring the scorched console panel from the experiment that had gone too far, I immersed myself in the energy logs, seeking patterns, something to anchor me in quantifiable reality. Something about the power fluctuations during the controlled tests nagged at me, a subtle anomaly my Watcher senses, even without the full calibration enhancement, couldn't ignore. Cross-referencing Path activation sequences with the city's main power grid readings and the deep-level sensors monitoring Xylos's geothermic core, I felt the familiar thrill of the hunt, focusing my scattered thoughts onto the data streams. This was the work I understood, the logic that cut through the chaos.

And then I found it. A distinct, alarming correlation. Every time we activated the Path, even at minimal yield, there was a corresponding, measurable energy drain not just from the immediate apparatus, but directly from the massive, central Weaving Crystal cluster deep beneath the city – the formation Zephyr and other Kryll occasionally referred to with quiet reverence as 'Scarabite-7'. It wasn't just resonance; it was consumption. The Path wasn't merely a bridge; it was a parasite, feeding on the very heart of Xylos. A terrifying, devastating truth.

I found Zephyr reviewing security footage in the command hub, his face illuminated by the shifting light of the displays, the lines of exhaustion etched deep around his eyes. "Zephyr," I began, my voice tight with the chilling implication of my discovery, cutting through the low hum of the command center. "The Path activations. They're drawing power directly from Scarabite-7. Significantly."

He didn't look surprised, merely turned from the screen, his expression grim, as if confirming a terrible suspicion. "Yes," he confirmed quietly, the word heavy with resignation. "I had suspected. The energy profiles were too closely matched for coincidence." He gestured towards a secondary display, activating a complex holographic projection showing swirling ancient Kryll script intertwined with stark energy flow diagrams – a visual representation of the knowledge he carried. "Our oldest texts speak of it," he explained, zooming in on a specific passage, the ancient glyphs swirling in the air between us. "They call the Nexus Path the 'Sky-Bridge' and warn that its use requires the 'Heartstone's Breath' – the energy of Scarabite-7."

He traced another line of flowing script with a fingertip, its meaning flickering uncertainly even in the translation matrix provided by Ma'at. "These same fragments speak of... others. Not the Collective, but races who navigated the Sky-Bridge long before Kryll consciousness even touched it. The 'Void Weavers,' the 'Star Singers'... names without faces, leaving only energetic echoes and warnings in the Path's currents." Zephyr's gaze grew distant, troubled, looking beyond the walls of the hub, into the vastness the Path hinted at. "Some passages hint the Great Mistake wasn't merely Kryll arrogance reaching too far within the Path, but an... encounter. An interaction with something ancient already dwelling within those currents, or perhaps something attracted by our initial, clumsy activations. The records are broken here, intentionally obscured by survivors, invoking concepts of 'Unraveling Light' and 'Silent Watchers Beyond.'" He pointed to another section of the main text, the warnings stark even in their fragmented form. "There are fragmented cautions against 'over-drawing the Wellspring', lest the 'World Shield' falter. Poetic ambiguities, until correlated with the energy data and these more terrifying fragments."

"You knew?" A surge of frustration, sharp and unwelcome, cut through my exhaustion. "You knew the Path might be consuming the very crystals that power your shields, that protect your world? And that it might hold... other things? That we could be draining your planet's lifeblood?"

"I suspected the power drain," he corrected, meeting my gaze directly, his eyes holding a weary honesty. "The nature of what else might reside within the Path, or who else might have trod it... that is the knowledge sealed away after the Mistake. I withheld confirmation until we had irrefutable proof of the energy link – your analysis provides that. To reveal such possibilities prematurely... the panic it would ignite, the potential for misuse by factions like Twelve, who seek power through any means... knowledge of this magnitude is a weapon in itself, Keket. I had to be certain before I shared this burden."

The silence stretched, thick with the terrifying weight of the confirmed drain. It wasn't just finding a resource anymore. This was about the lifeblood of a world, a power that consumed as it revealed, and the potential to awaken ancient, unknown forces. The scale of the threat had just expanded exponentially, drawing in not just the Collective and the Kryll, but potentially entities as old as the stars themselves. And it was our discovery, bound by the resonance between my tech and his world. My mission, my escape from the "ground static," had led me here, to potentially participate in the death of a planet. "We can't just take the Scarabite-7 now," I stated, the words heavy with the collapse of my original mission parameters, the practical goal replaced by existential dread. "Using the Path might kill your world. The very resource the Collective is desperate for is tied to your destruction, Zephyr. And potentially the awakening of whatever caused the Great Mistake." My mission had just become a thousand times more complicated, a thousand times more dangerous, irrevocably binding my fate to his and Xylos's.

Zephyr nodded grimly, his jaw tight. "And the Collective wants this resource," he added, his voice low. "They won't stop. If they force our shield down, if they breach the spire and reach the Heartstone without understanding... they could inadvertently drain Xylos themselves. Or worse, activate the Path without understanding, unleashing whatever our ancestors sealed away." His gaze was fixed on the tactical display showing the hulking Collective ship in orbit. "They are a threat, yes, but they are also a danger to themselves and the galaxy if they gain control over something they don't comprehend. We are trapped between a predictable, brutal force and unpredictable, ancient power, with Xylos as the prize and the victim." The implications solidified our precarious alliance, forging it not just in shared danger, but in the shared burden of this horrifying knowledge. The external threat of the Collective and the internal threat of Faction Twelve now seemed inextricably linked, circling this single, vulnerable point: the Heartstone, Scarabite-7, the Wellspring that the Path consumed. Every calculation changed.

Every decision about using the Path, about defending the city, about dealing with the Collective, now came with the chilling rider. At what cost to Xylos itself? We had to understand the drain, understand the Path's true nature, before any further action. Ignorance was no longer an option, but knowledge felt like a poisoned chalice, forcing agonizing choices at every turn.

A security report chimed, interrupting the heavy silence, pulling Zephyr back to the immediate crisis. He acknowledged it, his face tightening further, the brief glimpse of vulnerability vanishing behind the commander's mask. "The saboteurs near relay 4-Beta have been apprehended," he relayed, his voice flat, devoid of emotion. "Three members of Faction Twelve. The nutrient conduit sustained moderate damage during their capture; localized rationing will be necessary in that sector." The cost of his earlier 'acceptable damage' order made plain, a grim tally in the ongoing conflict. He accessed a restricted security file, displaying blurred images of the captured Kryll – young, faces set with grim fanaticism, eyes burning with conviction. "Interrogation protocols yielded little," Zephyr continued, his voice tight with frustration. "Standard Faction Twelve rhetoric – fear of outsiders, corruption of the Path, adherence to the 'pure' Kryll way, a return to ancient isolation." "They cling to fragmented texts from before the sealing, whispers of a 'pure' Kryll light untainted by the void. They see any interaction, any exchange, as a weakening." He paused, accessing deeper historical archives. "But one," he zoomed in on a specific transcript fragment filled with defiant clicks and whistles, translated as fragmented, radical pronouncements, "'Malakor'. Not a name in our current census." He frowned, the holographic display shifting to ancient lineage charts. "An archaic name. Associated with a lineage thought ended during the Great Mistake... one that advocated weaponizing the Path before it was sealed, seeing it not as a bridge but a weapon." Zephyr's expression tightened. This wasn't just general fear of outsiders driving Faction Twelve; it was a specific, ancient, and dangerous ideology re-emerging, seeking to control the very power we were now investigating – a political faction potentially armed with historical knowledge of how to misuse the Path. The implication hung in the air, chilling in its potential. Faction Twelve wasn't just driven by fear; they might be influenced by a resurrected, dangerous ideology, potentially led by someone claiming a lost, radical heritage, seeking to control the very power we were now investigating. This internal threat wasn't just about politics; it was tied directly to the very cosmic force we were exploring.

He turned off the report display, the cost of his earlier 'acceptable damage' order made plain, the weight of it settling visibly upon him. He looked at me, the mask of command slipping slightly, revealing the strain beneath, the weariness that mirrored my own. "A necessary price," he repeated, the words sounding hollow even to him, a justification that felt inadequate in the face of the human cost, both Kryll and Terran, visible around us. "Leadership, Keket... true leadership here, for generations... has often meant choosing between unavoidable harms. Selecting the path that preserves the whole, even if parts must suffer, even if the choice is agonizing." He gestured vaguely towards the city outside, the glowing spires a monument to their survival. "Our ancestors made terrible choices to shield this world from external threats and internal strife. They built this sanctuary, but its foundations rest on compromises that still haunt us, moral ambiguities woven into the very fabric of our existence." He paused, the vulnerability she'd glimpsed earlier resurfacing, raw and exposed. "Understanding the true cost of survival, the moral ambiguities woven into our very existence... It is a heavy burden. One I hesitated to inflict upon you, especially regarding Scarabite-7, until the truth was undeniable. Now... you carry it too." I stared at him, the weight of his words, his shared burden, settling over her like a physical cloak. He wasn't just the Protector of Xylos, the formidable warrior; at this moment, stripped of his command facade, he was achingly vulnerable, offering her the raw, bleeding truth of his world's deepest fear and its most dangerous secret. This sharing, she realized with a jolt that had nothing to do with energy fields, was an act of profound trust, perhaps even a quiet plea for an alliance that went far beyond strategic necessity. He was binding her to him, to Xylos, not with prophecies or duty, but with the stark, terrible beauty of a shared, impossible truth.

His words, the weight of his confession, landed heavily. The truth of Scarabite-7's consumption, the hidden ancient threats, the internal conflict—this wasn't just his burden anymore. It was ours, a shared secret tying us together in this escalating crisis.

I started from the damning energy graphs to Zephyr's weary, resolute face. The Path wasn't just a discovery; it was a poisoned chalice, a power that consumed the heart of this world and potentially awakened ancient, unknown forces. Zephyr wasn't just a commander; he was the inheritor of generations of morally grey survival, forced to make impossible choices in real-time, choices that had immediate, tangible consequences. Above, the Collective waited, a known, brutal threat. Within the city, dissent festered, willing to sabotage their own world out of fear and radical ideology. And the greatest secret, the power of Scarabite-7, was now revealed to be the potential instrument of their own destruction, and perhaps ours. The fragile hope the Nexus Path had offered felt suddenly, terrifyingly, like the edge of an abyss, a path paved with impossible choices and unimaginable risks, each one weighted by the drain on Xylos's heart.

The silence stretched between us, thick with the weight of the Scarabite-7 revelation and Zephyr's somber confession. The holographic displays cast complex, shifting shadows on our faces, illuminating the exhaustion etched deep around our eyes. The adrenaline that had fueled us through the ambush and the initial confrontation with the Collective had finally ebbed, leaving behind a profound weariness, bone-deep and mind-numbing. Zephyr looked away from the tactical maps, his gaze settling on me. He noted the slight tremor in my hands as I rested them on the console, the way I unconsciously rubbed my temples, the faint bruising still visible near my hairline from a near-miss during the ambush. He felt his own fatigue dragging at him, a leaden weight behind his eyes, the constant vigilance demanding a toll.

"The hour is late," he said, his voice softer now, stripped of command resonance, a simple statement of fact. "And the threats – external and internal – will still be here when the next cycle begins. Continued analysis without rest yields diminishing returns, and invites error. We need clear minds to face what comes next." He gestured slightly towards the exit. "Sustenance and rest are necessary. For both of us. We have faced enough for one cycle."

I nodded mutely. The thought of deciphering more ancient texts or analyzing complex energy signatures felt impossible right now. My mind felt saturated, unable to process another dire implication or strategic calculation. The primal needs – food, sleep – asserted themselves with sudden force, a basic, grounding reality in the face of cosmic uncertainty. Zephyr procured two compact ration packs from a nearby dispenser – nutrient-dense Kryll staples designed for efficiency, bland but necessary. Without further discussion, he followed me as I led the way through the now-quieter corridors back to my assigned quarters. The ambient light was low, most non-essential personnel presumably attempting some form of rest despite the oppressive tension radiating from the Collective ship hanging unseen above the shield. Guards still stood sentinel at key junctions, their alertness a stark reminder of the ongoing crisis, their faces grim in the dim light. Inside my small, functional room, the silence felt different – less charged with revelation, more filled with shared exhaustion. We sat, not at the small data terminal, but on simple floor cushions near a low table, the custom in many Kryll private spaces.

We ate the rations mostly in silence. The food was bland but nourishing, a dense paste with a slightly nutty flavor, sustenance without ceremony. The act of simply eating, performing a mundane, necessary function in the midst of an overwhelming crisis, felt strangely grounding, a small pocket of normalcy. I watched Zephyr over the rim of my water bulb. The commander's harsh lines had softened slightly in his fatigue. I saw the weariness in the slight slump of his shoulders, the way he rubbed the bridge of his nose between bites. He wasn't just a formidable leader or a figure of confusing intimacy; he was also carrying an immense, solitary burden, now slightly shared between us. He caught my gaze, and for a moment, there was a flicker of understanding that transcended words – an acknowledgment of the dangers faced, the terrible knowledge now between us, the precariousness of our situation, and the simple, shared need for respite. No demands, no expectations, just the quiet company of two beings pushed to their limits, facing impossible choices under an alien sky, bound by a dangerous secret.

When the rations were finished, the silence returned, heavy but no longer strained. The shared meal, the brief cessation of crisis-level thinking, had created a small pocket of calm in the storm, a fragile truce with the chaos. "Rest," Zephyr said finally, rising, the commander resurfacing just enough to signal the end of the brief truce with exhaustion. "We will need clear minds tomorrow to face what comes." He gave a slight, almost formal nod, his gaze lingering for a moment before he turned towards the exit. He exited my quarters, leaving me alone with the echo of his presence, the chilling secrets of Scarabite-7, the memory of his touch, and the daunting prospect of the cycle yet to come, and the impossible choices that awaited us. Sleep, I suspected, would still be a long time coming.

Chapter 16: The Choice and the Catalyst

Zephyr

The pre-dawn quiet of Xylos hummed, a fragile peace that did little to soothe the dissonant thrumming beneath my own skin – a resonance tuned solely to her. Keket. Even after the draining Path experiments, the confrontations, the raw, uncontrolled intensity of our first real kiss, the air around her still crackled, pulling at my senses. The unsettling hum beneath the city, the one tied to the Path and the potential ancient attention, felt louder now, a constant, low-frequency tremor against my control.

The intrusion, when it came, was brutal. The Collective's ultimatum – stark glyphs demanding her surrender, threatening my world – landed like a physical blow. Ice, sharp and cruel, pierced the low fire she ignited in me, replaced instantly by a white-hot protective rage. They would not have her. The thought was primal, absolute. My hands clenched, the familiar feel of my own energy coiling uselessly against such a distant, faceless threat.

Briefly conferring with the Elders confirmed the impossible calculus – defiance risked annihilation, compliance was unthinkable. Their fear, amplified by the news of internal sabotage revealed, was a palpable wave against my resolve. The Scarabite-7 depletion, the chilling knowledge that our shield's power source was finite and vulnerable, compounded the dread. Our greatest power was now our greatest liability. The stakes, already galactic, had just become existential for Xylos.

I found her near the spire, the faint emerald glow caressing the strong lines of her face, highlighting the stubborn set of her jaw. She had seen the message. The universe held its breath, waiting for her choice. My gaze traced the curve of her shoulder under the practical fabric of her uniform, the long column of her neck where faint blue lines of tech pulsed like captured starlight. Every instinct screamed to pull her behind me, shield her, hide her away where the Collective's grasping reach could never touch her.

"Zephyr," her voice, steady despite the gravity of the moment, drew my eyes back to hers. Those impossible green eyes, holding galaxies of determination.

Keket:

He stood before me, a statue of contained tension, his eyes dark with a storm I recognized in the depths of his own being. The Collective's ultimatum blazed in my mind, stark and cold. Give myself up, or they would take Zephyr's world by force. My skin felt too tight, my uniform a flimsy barrier against the converging threats. The knowledge gained from the Path's nature, its link to Scarabite-7, the drain on Xylos's life force, the potential for ancient, watching entities, the internal Kryll divisions – solidified into a single, terrible truth. My mission was no longer just a resource. It was about the survival of this vibrant, impossible world, tied irrevocably to the enigmatic warrior standing before me, and bound by a connection I barely understood.

The sterile efficiency of the Collective, the endless data streams, the calculated cruelty masked as strategy, the quiet suffocation of the life I was expected to live – it flashed behind my eyes. Compared to the raw, dangerous vitality of Xylos, the impossible connection I felt here, the chance for work that truly mattered... there was no choice, not really. The fear was a cold weight, but the yearning for purpose, for something real, was stronger. My alliance with Zephyr, forged in shared danger and terrifying intimacy, felt more real than my fading ties to the Collective. Surrendering meant handing the Collective the key to the Path, risking its misuse, potentially unleashing the very ancient forces Zephyr feared. It meant abandoning this chance to understand, to contribute to something that felt profoundly important. And it meant abandoning Zephyr. The thought struck her with the force of a physical blow. This warrior-prince, with his impossible world and the even more impossible connection they shared, had awakened something in me I hadn't known was dormant. A sense of purpose, yes, but also a fierce, unexpected tenderness, a desire to stand beside him, not just as an ally, but as... more. To turn her back now felt like betraying not just Xylos, but the most vital, terrifyingly real part of myself I had only just discovered.

"My path... is no longer with the Collective." Each word was a hammer blow against the ice around my heart. Stated clearly. Unequivocal. "I refuse their ultimatum. I stand with Xylos."

Zephyr

Air rushed into my lungs, a breath I hadn't known I was holding. Relief, so potent it was almost painful, loosened the knot tightening in my chest. She chose us. She chose me. I wanted to cross the space between us, feel the solid reality of her, inhale the unique scent that clung to her – ozone, distant stars, warm skin – anchor myself to her presence. But the leader's mask, the shield of generations, snapped back into place. "Your decision is acknowledged, Captain Keket," I managed, my voice betraying none of the tumultuous relief flooding my senses.

Now, survival. The Collective waited. Faction Twelve lurked within the city. The Scarabite-7 was draining. Strategy dictated a desperate gamble: a controlled demonstration of the Nexus Path. Hoping to create a deterrent. Gain vital intelligence. A terrifying prospect after the chaotic surge and the unsettling echoes since. The risks were astronomical to Xylos, to the dwindling Scarabite-7, to us. But understanding the Path, how to control it, felt like our only weapon against all converging threats.

We stood before the spire again, the air thick with anticipation and the memory of our last chaotic connection. The crystals pulsed, their hum a counterpoint to the frantic beat of my own heart. "Absolute synchronization," I explained, the words feeling inadequate. "Total vulnerability." I looked at her, truly looked. At the pulse beating faintly at the base of her throat, the slight flush on her high cheekbones, the way she met my gaze without flinching. Revealing the next part felt like stripping myself bare. "This depth of merging... Keket, it echoes our most ancient bonding rituals." I saw the flicker in her eyes – surprise, perhaps apprehension. "Rituals meant to identify... true resonance. True Mates." Fear, cold and sharp, twisted inside me. Would she think this a trap? A coercion veiled in mysticism? "The ritual aspect is secondary," I forced out, needing her to believe it, needing it to be true for her sake. "The vulnerability is necessary for control. Only that." I stepped closer then, driven by a need that transcended strategy or prophecy. Her scent filled my senses, clouding my thoughts. My voice dropped, roughened by the raw truth. "But understand this, Keket. Path or no path, ritual or no ritual... My commitment is to you. If you choose the stars again... I would follow. If you stay..." My gaze locked with hers, conveying the desperate intensity I couldn't fully voice, the terrifying sincerity of a feeling that threatened to unravel everything his life had been built upon. "My need is for you." The words were a raw, exposed truth, a challenge to destiny and duty, a silent vow offered in the face of galactic conflict.

Her answering nod, the unwavering trust in her eyes, sent a tremor through me. We reached for each other, hands clasping. The energy surged, but this time I wrestled it, guided it with ancient chants murmured under my breath, weaving patterns of light and intent learned at my ancestors' knee. Her mind opened to mine, a landscape of sharp intelligence, fierce loyalty, and that core of restless fire. Vulnerability felt less like exposure, more like... completion.

Instability erupted – a jarring external probe, the Collective testing our shields? Energy lashed out from the spire. Without thought, I yanked Keket behind me, shielding her body with mine, absorbing the searing backlash into my own energy field. Pain ripped through me, but beneath it, the feel of her pressed against my back, the shared pulse of the connection, the absolute trust flowing between us... it was an anchor stronger than any crystal. We weathered the storm, the energy stabilizing, leaving a shimmering signature in the air.

Keket:

The surge hit. Controlled, this time, by Zephyr's will and the focused energy of the spire, but still immense. Images flashed, brief and contained – not the chaotic maelstrom of Chapter 8, but focused glimpses. The vastness of space. The humming network of the Path. And a fleeting, chilling sense of something... observing. The "Silent Watchers Beyond" from Chapter 10, a terrifying confirmation that our earlier, uncontrolled access had indeed drawn attention. Then, the sharp, jarring sensation of an external probe hitting the shield, coinciding precisely with the peak of the energy surge. A direct attack. The Collective. My tech screamed data overlays – shield harmonics stressed, unusual energy frequencies detected from above.

Before I could process the external threat, pain lanced through me. Zephyr. He had pulled me behind him, shielding me from a backlash of energy from the spire. His body is a solid, protective barrier against the raw force. The scent of ozone and his unique, grounding energy filled my senses. My hand, still clasped in his, felt the tremor in his fingers, the strain in his muscles as he absorbed the impact. Trust, forged in crisis, solidified in that moment.

Zephyr

Still holding her hand, feeling the fine bones beneath her warm skin, I opened the Collective channel. "Sah Collective Command," my voice rang with newfound, absolute authority. Tempered by the chilling awareness of what we had just glimpsed, what we might have alerted. "Ultimatum rejected." I declared

Keket under Xylos's protection, invoked the K'Tharr Accords, hinted at the power they had just witnessed – the shimmering signature of the controlled Path energy hanging visible in the air. "Withdraw."

Silence, then the severed connection. A reprieve. For now. The immediate tension broke, leaving exhaustion and the vibrating awareness between us. I looked at Keket, truly saw her – the smudge of crystal dust on her cheek, the way adrenaline still sparked in her eyes, the undeniable pull she exerted on my very being. She had chosen my world. I needed to share it with her. Needed the release. Needed... more.

"Let me show you Xylos beyond these walls," I offered, the idea taking shape. A moment of shared escape amidst the storm. "My Light Runner. Come."

The sleek black pilot suits felt like second skin. Seeing Keket in hers... the form-fitting material emphasized the lean strength of her body, the curve of her hips, the length of her legs. My breath caught. Focus, Zephyr. I swung onto the Runner, the familiar machine humming beneath me. She climbed on behind, her movements fluid, graceful even in the unfamiliar gear. Her hands came to rest on my waist, hesitant at first. The contact sent a jolt straight through me, far more potent than any energy surge.

Then we flew. The city blurred into rivers of light. Wind screamed past, carrying the electric tang of the air, the mineral scent of the deep city, and beneath it all, the intoxicating fragrance that was purely Keket, intensified by our proximity. I pushed the Runner, weaving through transit lanes with practiced ease, feeling the powerful engine vibrate through my bones, feeling her body pressed firmly against my back, her thighs alongside mine. Her initial hesitation vanished, replaced by tightening hands on my waist. Her chest pressed against my shoulder blades as she leaned with me into a tight curve. I felt the vibration of her surprised laugh against my skin, a sound that resonated deeper than any crystal hum. Adrenaline surged, sharpened by her closeness, by the undeniable friction, the heat of her body against mine. Every nerve ending felt alive, attuned to her presence, the simple act of piloting transformed into an intense, sensory ballet. The wanting, the physical ache I'd been suppressing, roared to life, fueled by speed and proximity and the sheer, undeniable fact of her.

I brought the Runner to a smooth halt on a high, quiet platform overlooking the glowing city. The engine died, leaving only the soft thrum of Xylos and the sound of our mingled breathing in the sudden stillness. Her hands lingered on my waist for a beat longer than necessary before slowly releasing. The space she left felt cold. The adrenaline was fading, leaving behind the raw, vibrating hum of our connection, amplified by the shared thrill. We didn't speak. We didn't need to. Her choice, the Path, the Collective threat – it all waited. But in the wake of the ride, under the watchful glow of my city, the air between us shimmered with a different kind of energy, a tension that promised consequences far more personal, and infinitely more consuming, than any galactic ultimatum. The controlled Path demonstration was a success, for now. But the price... The Drain was real. The ancient Watchers were real. And the fight had just begun.

Chapter 17: Weaving New Paths Towards Connection

Keket

The pale, alien light of Xylos filtered through the viewport of my quarters aboard the Celestial Barque. Morning. Or whatever passed for it on this world perpetually bathed in the glowing energy shield that had just repelled a Collective dreadnought and was constantly tested by internal saboteurs. Last cycle's... resolution... echoed in the unusual quiet. Zephyr's declaration, the shaky ceasefire after the tense standoff in relief warred with ingrained suspicion. Can I truly trust this sudden shift from outright aggression and veiled threats to an invitation for peace? My mind, trained for the cold calculus of command and negotiation, replayed his words, his stance, the flicker of something vulnerable I thought I'd glimpsed in those luminous white eyes during the Path demonstration and the tension. Was it a calculated move to gain control? Or genuine exhaustion and a strategic necessity born from the shared threat of the Collective and the chilling discovery of the Scarabite-7 drain revealed just cycles ago? With the Kryll, the line felt impossibly blurred, a dangerous uncertainty I had to navigate for my crew's safety.

A chime broke the silence, the specific, melodic tone designated for Zephyr, bypassing standard comms. My comm panel lit up. "Keket." His voice, resonant even through the speaker, lacked the hard edge of command it held yesterday. The raw vulnerability I'd felt in his touch during the Path demonstration, the desperation in his kiss... it was etched into the timbre of his voice.

"I trust you rested adequately."

"As well as circumstances allowed, Zephyr," I replied, keeping my tone neutral, professional, mirroring his. The weight of command pressed down, reminding me I was Captain first, guest second, and whatever else had passed between us was a perilous complication.

"Good. To solidify our agreement, I extend a formal invitation. Not merely to you, but to your senior officers – Sekem, Bastet, others you deem essential. Leave the Barque. Be guests within the city. Within my spire."

My breath hitched. Inside? Not just contained, but welcomed? This wasn't just political maneuvering; this was a profound gesture of trust on his part, demanding an equal leap from mine. It was also a strategic opportunity – to gain intelligence, understand their society from within, secure my key officers from the vulnerable orbital position, exposed as we were to the Collective's whim. But the risk... placing ourselves willingly within the heart of his power, a power now known to draw from the vulnerable Scarabite-7 and possibly linked to ancient, volatile forces like the "Silent Watchers Beyond" hinted at... It's a bigger leap than crossing the void. A necessary leap, though, if we were to truly understand the Path and survive the coming storm.

"Your offer is... significant, Zephyr," I said carefully, choosing my words. "A demonstration of good faith I cannot ignore. It also presents strategic advantages for my crew's disposition given the current orbital threats." My mind raced, assessing my team. Sekem would be stoic, following orders but constantly vigilant. Bastet, wary but loyal, her brilliant engineering mind already buzzing with questions about this impossible city's structure and energy. Joric, ever watchful, would catalog every guard, every exit. They trusted my lead, even when it felt like I was navigating a minefield blindfolded, relying on an alien leader whose motivations were still shrouded in layers of history and recent, confusing intimacy.

"We accept. Inform me of the protocols."

"Excellent. Preparations are underway. Expect departure coordinates shortly." The connection clicked off. I took a steadying breath, the recycled air of my ship suddenly feeling stale, constricting. I relayed the orders.

Sekem's acknowledgement was clipped, efficient. Bastet, however, sounded less composed. "Acknowledged, Captain. But..." Her voice trailed off for a fraction longer than usual, her concern palpable even over the internal comm, a pragmatic engineer facing the utterly inexplicable. "...we're leaving the ship? With the Collective up there? Are you sure about this?" she finally asked, before confirming. My closeness to Zephyr, my trust in his word, was clearly putting a strain on my crew's faith, leaving them vulnerable and confused.

"Understood, Bastet," I said, trying to project calm reassurance. "Maintain strict radio silence on your approach. Stay alert. Report any anomalies on the ground. Keket out." The low hum of the ship's systems seemed louder now, a counterpoint to the silence from Collective space – a silence that felt increasingly heavy, hinting at the worsening galactic situation and the Collective's potential desperation, a tension I'd felt building since Chapter 11.

Leaving the Barque felt like shedding a skin, leaving behind my command center, my solid, understandable world of steel and vacuum. The familiar clang of the docking ramp retracting, the hum of my engines fading, replaced by the whisper of Kryll transports arriving. Stepping out onto Xylos proper, into the designated transport, was stepping into another reality, one defined by alien energy and fragile trust.

And we arrived at the spire. It wasn't a building, not in any human sense. It rose towards the shielded sky like a colossal, living crystal, light pulsing softly within its walls. Structures flowed, curved, devoid of sharp corners, interwoven with panels that shifted with gentle luminescence and strands of glowing, bioluminescent flora I couldn't name. Walls weren't truly solid; they seemed semi-translucent, offering hazy, distorted views of the city or the artificial sky beyond. Not stone and steel, but light and life woven together, powered by the very Scarabite-7 we now knew was being consumed by the Path. Ancient, yet impossibly advanced, a monument to Kryll resilience and vulnerability. Like living inside a geode touched by starlight and built on a ticking clock. A low, pervasive hum resonated through the structure, felt more than heard – the city's heartbeat, steady and controlled, but knowing its energy source was finite now added a layer of tension to its song. Occasionally, soft, chime-like notes drifted on the air currents, perhaps the crystalline structure itself singing, or communicating. The air smelled impossibly clean, sharp with ozone, tinged with the metallic scent of exotic minerals and the subtle, sweet fragrance of the alien vegetation integrated into the walls. It smells like power contained... and finite.

Zephyr met us in the entrance hall. He moved with a fluid grace that seemed amplified in his own environment, less the rigid warrior I'd first encountered, more the master of his domain, the Protector in his element. He inclined his head, a gesture less deferential, more welcoming, his luminous eyes sweeping over my officers, assessing. "Welcome to Xylos Prime Spire."

He guided us through corridors that seemed to breathe light, an unsettling but captivating display of his people's mastery over energy and crystal. I watched Sekem's impassive face, his gaze subtly cataloging security details. Bastet's wide eyes taking everything in, undoubtedly calculating energy flows and structural integrity with her Earth-trained engineering brain and finding it defy all logic, the frustration of an engineer facing the inexplicable palpable. Joric, ever watchful, would catalog every guard, every exit, his stance radiating a quiet vigilance that reassured me my security chief was assessing the environment for the internal threats Zephyr and I knew lurked in the shadows after the ambush. Rooms were assigned – elegant, minimalist spaces defined by curved walls, glowing light panels, and furniture that looked grown rather than built. Comfort, undeniably, but alien. Nothing felt familiar, underscoring our status as outsiders, guests in a potentially volatile sanctuary.

This is his power base. His home, I thought, was a place built on centuries of survival and secret knowledge. Seeing this... it changes the scale of him. He's not just a warrior prince; he's the heart of this world, its strength and its vulnerability embodied. The alliance felt heavier, more real, standing here within his walls, seeing the world he carried the weight of.

Later, I did a quick check-in with my senior officers via internal comm before the scheduled dinner with Zephyr. "All settled, Captain," Sekem reported, his voice as impassive as ever, a solid anchor of Terran normalcy amidst the alienness. Bastet, however, sounded less composed. "Settled, yes, Captain. But this place..." I could almost hear her brilliant, pragmatic engineer frowning, struggling with the sheer impossibility of it all. "The energy signatures are off the charts, obviously, but the control systems... it's all interwoven, organic. Trying to interface our standard diagnostic tools feels like trying to plug a hydro-spanner into a tree. It's defying fundamental principles of energy transfer and structural load I learned at the Academy. I don't trust tech I can't isolate and quantify, Captain. This 'living crystal' feels less like stable engineering and more like... well, like something that could decide to stop working if it gets offended. Especially if its power source is... being drained, as you suspected." Her voice dropped on the last part, a quiet acknowledgement of the terrifying data from Chapter 15.

"Understood, Bastet," I replied, a small, grim smile touching my lips. "Maintain standard diagnostics where possible, log any anomalies, but tread carefully. We're guests... in a very powerful, potentially temperamental house," I finished, echoing her own earlier sentiment from Chapter 11. Her ingrained engineering skepticism was a vital counterpoint to the alien elegance, grounding our presence here in practical concerns despite the escalating cosmic weirdness.

After ensuring my crew was settled, Zephyr sought me out again. He found me observing the cityscape from a crystalline balcony, the lights below swirling like captive nebulae, a breathtaking, impossible sight that momentarily eased the tension.

"Keket." His voice was closer now, devoid of any electronic filter, cutting through the spire's ambient hum.

"My senior staff will ensure your officers are attended to," he said, his posture relaxed, but the coiled tension remained beneath the surface. The weight of his responsibilities, the recent confrontations, were etched in the subtle lines around his eyes, visible even in the soft light. "I request the pleasure of your company for a private dinner this evening. To... discuss our path forward." Just me? Why? Professional obligation – the need to understand the Scarabite-7 drain, the Path, his people's politics – warred with a flicker of something else – curiosity, a strange pull that had nothing to do with strategy. Our path forward. He saw us as intertwined now, bound by shared secrets and a dangerous key.

"A private dinner seems appropriate," I agreed, keeping my voice steady, acknowledging the strategic necessity of the meeting.

"Before that," he gestured towards an internal garden bathed in soft, golden light, an unexpected sanctuary within the living crystal, "perhaps a walk? The spire can feel confining initially."

We walked in silence for a time, the only sounds were the soft hum of the spire and the whisper of his robes against the crystalline floor. The garden was filled with impossible plants – flora that pulsed with soft light, vines dripping what looked like liquid silver, flowers that opened and closed like breathing organisms. The air here was thick with perfume – heavier, sweeter than outside, cloying but captivating. The tension between us was a palpable thing, an invisible current in the air, amplified by the knowledge of the shared danger, the shared secrets, the raw intimacy of the lab. I was acutely aware of his presence beside me, tall and imposing even without his armor, a being who seemed as intrinsically linked to this place as the crystal walls themselves.

I watched the light play across the sharp planes of his obsidian face, the way his stark white hair seemed to almost glow, a stark, alien beauty that was undeniably captivating. He walks like a predator, I thought, contained but always aware, a protector in every step. As he turned slightly to point out a particular bloom, he passed close.His scent hit me – not just the clean ozone of the spire, but something personal, intrinsic. Rain dew. Damp earth. A surprising hint of something warm and woody, like vanilla, but deeper. Wilder. It's... grounding, I realized with a jolt. Unexpectedly pleasant. My reaction was involuntary, a sharp intake of breath. Did he notice? My own scent felt suddenly loud in the enclosed space. But then, as I moved past him to examine the flower, I saw his nostrils flare almost imperceptibly. His luminous eyes flickered towards me, a momentary intensity in their depths. Did he notice? My own scent – the subtle fruit and cashmere wood notes of my preferred Terran toiletries – felt suddenly loud in the enclosed space, an unwelcome intrusion into the alien environment and the heightened awareness between us. That small, almost-missed exchange sent a jolt through me, tightening the strange awareness between us. This is dangerous territory, my mind screamed. Keep it professional. Analyze, don't react. But my pulse was hammering against my ribs, betraying the cool professionalism I strived for.

The private dining area was breathtaking, overlooking the glowing expanse of the city through a vast, curved crystalline wall. The table itself was polished crystal, subtle patterns of light dancing across its surface. Minimalist, elegant, intimate. Isolated from the rest of the spire, political machinations and external threats. A place designed for focused conversation, for peeling back layers. Zephyr had changed. He wore flowing robes of deep cobalt, intricately woven with threads that seemed to capture the ambient light. Less the weapon, more the prince, but the coiled power was still there, visible in the breadth of his shoulders, the defined muscles hinted at beneath the fabric. His obsidian skin seemed to drink the light, while his white hair was a startling, luminous contrast. His voice, when he spoke, was calmer, the melodic Kryll cadence clearer without the tension of conflict, making the alien language feel less foreign, more like a natural part of this world's hum.

Food was an assault on the senses. Vibrant colours – purples, greens, blues I'd never seen in nature. Unfamiliar shapes arranged with artistic precision. The scents were complex: spicy, floral, earthy, utterly alien, yet my calibrated senses processed them with a growing appreciation for their complexity. I cautiously tried a segment of a deep purple fruit. The taste exploded on my tongue –

echoes of passion fruit and dragon fruit, but sharper, wilder. Alien, yet delicious, a taste of true discovery. A crystalline carafe held a glowing blue liquid. Kryll wine, Zephyr explained. It was smooth, deceptively potent, warming me faster than expected, sharpening my senses further, blurring the edges of my analytical mind.

As we ate, he initiated the sharing. He spoke of his past, his voice losing some of its regal formality, revealing the man beneath the commander. His parents, killed during the chaos of the Great Mistake, before the city's shield was perfected. It added a layer of understanding to his fierce protectiveness, his caution, and the terrible weight of responsibility he carried for this city's survival. He mentioned brothers – a fleeting reference that hinted at complex family dynamics, potential political heirs or rivals, adding another layer to the political landscape and the weight of his position. He spoke of the burden of the Protector lineage, the constant vigilance, the isolation inherent in knowing the secrets of the Path and the true vulnerability of their shielded world. It wasn't just duty; it was a life shaped by loss and the terrifying knowledge of what lay hidden beneath the surface, making the simple act of sharing a meal, of finding a flicker of understanding with an outsider, feel both perilous and profoundly desired. He confirmed his position, not just Prince or Protector, but commander of Xylos's primary defense force, the largest military power on the planet. He's showing trust, I analyzed. Calculated honesty? Or genuine openness? A flicker of empathy stirred within me for the burden he carried, the weight of his people's survival and past traumas etched into his being. This wasn't just a political leader; this was a man shaped by loss and impossible responsibility, choosing to reveal himself.

Then it was my turn. Equal footing requires equal vulnerability... carefully measured. I chose my words, sharing carefully selected details about my parents, their roles high within OmniCorp and PetroMax Interstellar – the corporate behemoths that had shaped my early life, the source of the "ground static" I'd fled.I spoke of the philosophical differences, the stifling expectations that drove me to seek my own path among the stars. A path away from the 'ground static' of profit margins and calculated losses, towards something unknown, challenging, where my work might feel real. This desperate search for meaning was the engine that drove me across the void, a stark contrast to the deep, rooted connection Zephyr had to Xylos. I watched him as I spoke, trying to gauge his reaction. Does he understand the cutthroat empires I navigated? Does he see the fundamental difference between their drive for pure profit and the Kryll fight for survival and harmony? He listened intently, his luminous eyes fixed on mine, seeming to absorb not just my words but the unspoken motivations beneath them – the blend of rebellion, duty, and restless longing that defined me. And as I spoke of the emptiness I'd sought to fill among the stars," Keket continued, her voice softening, "I saw something shift in his gaze – not just understanding, but a flicker of profound recognition, an echo of his own burdens. He reached across the table, his fingers lightly brushing mine as he refilled my crystal cup with the glowing blue wine. The touch was brief, almost accidental, yet the warmth lingered, a silent acknowledgment of the dangerous, fragile bridge they were building between their vastly different souls, here in the heart of his alien world.

Throughout the meal, the tension remained, a high-frequency hum beneath the surface of the conversation. I caught him watching me, his gaze intense, holding something more than polite interest, something that resonated with the unexpected connection we'd forged. I forced my own eyes away, only to find them lingering moments later on the strong line of his jaw, the elegant, deliberate movement of his hands as he gestured. Stop staring. The quiet of the room amplified everything – the soft clink of unfamiliar utensils against crystal, our synchronized breathing during pauses, the frantic beat of my own pulse in my ears. Charged silences stretched, heavy with unspoken thoughts. I felt the warmth radiating from a nearby light panel, the cool smoothness of the crystal cup in my hand, but mostly, I felt him. The awareness of the space between us felt like static electricity, crackling, ready to arc. There was no point denying it anymore. The attraction was strong, undeniable. Physical, yes – his presence was overwhelming, beautiful in a stark, alien way that defied human standards. That imposing physique, the contrast of dark skin and white hair, the intensity in those eyes... But it was becoming tangled now with the respect I was starting to feel, the awareness of the power he wielded so carefully, the vulnerability he'd just shown by sharing his history and his burden. It's... complicated, I admitted to myself. And incredibly dangerous. Not just the situation, but the undeniable pull between us. The shared secrets, the near-death experiences, the clash of our cultures, the growing understanding forged in this crucible – it all converged in the charged silence. It wasn't just physical attraction; it was the terrifying intimacy of being truly seen, truly understood, in a way neither of us had experienced before, amplifying the already high stakes of our alliance and the unknown nature of the bond.

The meal concluded. Conversation lulled. A fragile sense of intimacy hung in the air, built on shared words and unveiled histories, forged in the crucible of shared danger and profound, terrifying discoveries. We built something tonight, I thought. Trust, understanding... attraction. But the awareness remained, thick and unresolved, amplified by the subtle hum of the spire, the distant echo of the Scarabite-7, the unseen threat of the Collective. And I felt it – there was still something more, something held back, something that tied the personal to the galactic in ways I didn't yet understand.

Zephyr's gaze held mine across the polished crystal table, intense, searching, mirroring the unspoken awareness that hung thick between us. The air crackled, amplified by the shared history, the quiet meal, the isolation of the private dining space. He didn't speak the line about "something more" yet. Instead, his hand reached across the table, not for my hand, but cupping my jaw gently, his touch surprisingly warm against my skin. "Come," he murmured, his voice low, resonant, a simple request that felt heavy with implication, with the weight of the moment and the night ahead. "Let us continue this... elsewhere. My private suite." He rose slowly, not waiting for an answer I couldn't have given anyway, his gaze holding mine, pulling me out of my analytical mind and into the present.

He led me out of the private dining area, his hand a warm, solid anchor on my arm, the simple contact sending a familiar, unsettling jolt through me. The corridors of the spire seemed different at this hour, quieter, lit with softer, ambient glows, feeling less like public passages and more like arteries leading to a hidden core. We passed a few guards, who inclined their heads respectfully to Zephyr, their gazes flicking to me with veiled curiosity before returning to their posts. He led me through passages that felt increasingly personal, less public, until we arrived before a seamless section of crystalline wall that pulsed with a subtle golden light. He placed his palm against it, and the wall shimmered, dilating inward with a soft whisper, revealing not another corridor, but a spacious, self-contained suite. "My private quarters," he stated simply, gesturing me inside. The air here was warmer, carrying a faint, personal scent I now associated uniquely with him – that grounding mix of rain dew, damp earth, and wild vanilla. The space was large, defined by the same elegant, curved crystalline architecture as the rest of the spire, but furnished for comfort and solitude. A large, plush sleeping platform dominated one section, covered in soft, dark fabrics. Panels in the walls shifted with mesmerizing, soothing light patterns. It felt like a sanctuary within a sanctuary, a place of vulnerability and potential. He followed me in, the wall sealing behind us with a soft thud that cut us off from the rest of the spire, from the city under siege, from the Barque in orbit, from the Collective above, from the world outside. He turned to me, his eyes dark with the same intense awareness that mirrored my own. I knew the delicate balance we had maintained was about to shift irrevocably. The wall whispered shut behind us, sealing us within the warmth and quiet of his private quarters. The air, scented faintly with that grounding mix of rain dew, damp earth, and wild vanilla that was uniquely him, felt thick with anticipation, charged with the unspoken possibilities of the night. He didn't move immediately, just stood there, his eyes, dark and luminous in the soft light, holding mine with an intensity that stole my breath. The elegant cobalt robes draped his frame, hinting at the power and grace beneath, a stark contrast to the rigid armor I'd first seen him in, a visual echo of the layers he'd peeled back tonight, revealing the man beneath the commander.

My pulse hammered against my ribs, a frantic drumbeat against the steady, almost silent hum of the spire. The private dinner, the shared histories, the careful dance of vulnerability – it had all led here. To this room, this moment, this undeniable pull between us that had nothing and everything to do with galactic stakes and ancient prophecies. He took a step towards me, slow and deliberate, and I held my ground, rooted to the spot, unable to look away, wanting him to close the distance.

When he reached me, he didn't speak. His hand came up, large and warm, cupping my cheek, his long fingers brushing softly against my skin, tracing the line of my jaw. A wave of heat spread through me, loosening the last of my carefully maintained composure, making my skin tingle with awareness. His eyes, so close now, searched mine. I saw not just desire, but a depth of need, a vulnerability that mirrored the ache in my own chest, a yearning that resonated with my own hidden loneliness. He lowered his head, slowly, giving me every opportunity to pull away, but the thought never even formed. I lifted my own hand, my palm resting against the warmth of his chest, feeling the strong, steady beat of his heart beneath the soft fabric of his robe.

His lips were soft against mine at first, a tentative brush that sent shivers through me, a whisper of what was to come. Then, the kiss deepened, gentleness giving way to a hunger that was both intoxicating and terrifying. I tangled my fingers in his thick, startlingly white hair, drawing him closer, losing myself in the heat and sensation, the alien texture of his hair soft against my fingertips. He tasted of the alien wine, of the shared vulnerability, of the promise of something wild and unknown. His arms came around me, strong and possessive, one hand finding the small of my back and pressing me flush against his body until there was no space left between us, only the electric awareness of skin meeting skin through the thin fabric, of two worlds colliding in the quiet sanctuary of his rooms. His other hand moved lower, tracing the curve of my hip, his touch sending a wave of pure physical sensation through me. This wasn't protocol. This wasn't science. This was the dangerous, exhilarating heart of the unknown, and I plunged into it headfirst, molding my body against his, feeling the hard lines of his muscles, the undeniable heat radiating from him, wanting more, needing more of this raw, grounding connection.

He broke the kiss, his breath coming in ragged gasps, and lifted me into his arms. I wrapped my legs around his waist instinctively, my uniform skirt riding high against his hips. He carried me across the room to the large, plush sleeping platform, its soft dark fabric illuminated by the gentle shifting light panels lined with opal stones. He lowered me onto the platform, his body following mine, pinning me gently beneath his weight. My hands went to the closures on my uniform shirt, fumbling with them. He helped, his fingers surprisingly adept, pulling the fabric away from my skin. I shrugged out of the shirt, the cool air hitting my bare shoulders, then the heat of his hands as they swept over my skin. My tank top was next, pulled over my head, leaving me bare to the waist.

He shed his own robes, the soft cobalt fabric pooling around him, revealing the full glory of his alien form. My breath hitched. He was breathtaking. The intricate, glowing patterns on his skin pulsed with a soft, internal light, tracing paths over dark, taut muscle. The texture of his skin, that beautiful mosaic of smooth areas and fine scales, was even more stunning without the barrier of his robes. He was warm, so incredibly warm to the touch, radiating a heat that seeped into my chilled skin. My hands explored him, tracing the lines of his shoulders, the planes of his chest, feeling the raw power humming beneath the surface, my fingers dancing over the glowing patterns, feeling the subtle energy there.

He lowered his head, his mouth finding the hollow of my throat, then trailing lower, tracing a path down my sternum, leaving a trail of fire in its wake. My head fell back against the soft platform, giving him access. He found the curve of my breast, his mouth warm and wet against my sensitive skin. He suckled gently at first, then with more urgency, sending waves of pleasure through me, making my hips instinctively arch off the platform. His tongue traced lazy circles around my nipple before taking it into his mouth, tugging and teasing, driving me wild. My hands tangled in his hair, holding him close, whispering sounds I didn't recognize.

While his mouth worked magic on my breasts, his hands moved lower, finding the waistband of my skirt. He fumbled with the closure, then pushed the fabric down my hips, past my thighs, leaving me bare below the waist. The cool air of the room hit my sensitive skin, only to be replaced by the heat of his hands as they swept over my legs, tracing the curve of my calves, the line of my thighs. He nudged my legs wider, settling between them, his body heat a furnace against my core.

He shifted, kneeling between my thighs, his luminous eyes burning into mine. His hands cupped my hips, tilting them slightly, positioning me. His breath was warm against the sensitive skin of my inner thighs, making me tremble in anticipation. He leaned down, his mouth finding my heat, his tongue tasting me, exploring with a slow, deliberate intensity that sent a jolt of pure pleasure through me. He suckled gently at first, then with more urgency, using his tongue and lips to tease and torment, driving me closer and closer to the edge. My fingers tangled in his hair, pulling him closer, arching my back, offering myself fully to his ministrations. He alternated between strong, deep strokes of his tongue and delicate flicks, finding every sensitive point, making me cry out his name, my body tightening with building pleasure.

When I was shaking and breathless, right on the edge of climax, he pulled back, rising to his feet. His gaze burned into mine, dark with shared pleasure and anticipation. He quickly shed the rest of his own clothing, his erection thick and hard, glistening in the soft light. My gaze traced the contours of his alien body, taking in the lean strength, the unique texture of his skin, the sheer physical reality of him.

He positioned himself between my spread thighs, nudging gently, finding my entrance. I was wet and ready, aching for him. With a low groan, he began to push. Slowly at first, his muscles tensed, his breath held. I felt the stretch, the fullness, the impossible reality of him filling me. My body adjusted, opening to accommodate his alien form. Then, he was fully buried inside me, deep and solid, a perfect, impossible fit. A wave of pure sensation washed over me, so intense it made my vision swim. I gripped his shoulders, my nails digging into his skin, anchoring myself to him in this physical reality.

He started to move, a slow, powerful rhythm that quickly built in intensity. His hips surged against mine, his body lifting and falling with each thrust. The friction, the heat, the sheer *rightness* of his body moving inside mine consumed my awareness. My consciousness narrowed to this point of connection, this impossible merging of human and alien, flesh and scale, starlight and planetary core. Each thrust was a wave of pure pleasure, building higher and higher. My breath came in ragged gasps, my body tightening around him, urging him faster. His hands moved to my hips, gripping them tightly, controlling the angle, deepening the penetration with each powerful stroke.

The glowing patterns on his skin pulsed brighter, mirroring the frantic beat of his heart against my chest. His skin felt slick with sweat under my hands as I raked my fingers through his hair, pulling his head down for a desperate, open-mouthed kiss. The taste of him, raw and wild, filled my mouth. There were no more thoughts, no more fears, only sensation. The world outside this embrace ceased to exist. It was just him, and me, and this raw, elemental act of connection in the sanctuary of his private rooms. My body tensed, building towards a peak, the pleasure sharp and intense. I cried out, my orgasm ripping through me, sending tremors through my limbs, my body convulsing around him.

He groaned, a guttural sound of release, and his thrusts quickened, becoming more frantic. His body stiffened, and I felt his own release hot and thick deep inside me. He collapsed against me, his weight heavy, his body shaking slightly with the aftershocks of his climax. His head rested against my shoulder, his breath coming in ragged gasps. We lay tangled together, slick with sweat, bodies intimately joined, the soft light of the spire casting a warm glow over our forms. The impossible reality of what had just happened, the depth of connection we had found, settled over us in the quiet aftermath. This wasn't just sex. It was a collision. A merging. A profound, terrifying, and utterly exhilarating confirmation of a bond that went beyond anything I could understand, forged in shared secrets and the quiet intimacy of the night. Bodies still tangled, breath soft against damp skin, a new silence settled. Not the charged tension of the lab, but a quiet awe. His hand, still warm against my back, tightened slightly. A silent question. A statement, <...*My love*...>. The thought, raw and clear, wasn't spoken aloud, but resonated in the space our bond created, a profound understanding passing between our joined minds. <... *Always*...>, my response, equally felt. A surrender. A promise. This wasn't just a connection. It was the core of everything.

Chapter 18: Harmonies Forged in Starlight

Keket:

In the wake of the revelations, the air in the crystal spire's resonant chamber was thick with unspoken words and lingering heat. The echoes of tested boundaries and fragile trust hummed beneath the surface of my thoughts as I prepared for this. We were here, drawn back by the higher calling of understanding the Path, the secrets of Scarabite-7, and the looming threat of the Collective and the lurking danger of Faction Twelve. But the decision to use our personal connection – our growing bond, forged in shared vulnerability and culminating in the kiss and the quiet understanding in as the anchor for this volatile power felt less like a scientific protocol and more like a leap of faith taken hand-in-hand after navigating bewildering intimacy. The fate of Xylos, perhaps more, rested on this.

Zephyr stood before the central console, the intricate patterns on his arms shimmering faintly, a visual echo of the spire's own internal light. The commander was present, yes, his posture radiating control, a shield against the immense pressure he carried. But so was the being who had shared the terrifying beauty of the void with me, whose touch had unlocked something fundamental, whose scent still lingered in my senses, whose unspoken words, "My need is for you", echoed in the quiet chamber.

"Absolute synchronization," Zephyr said in a lower tone, almost reverent, resonating with the chamber's hum, cutting through my lingering thoughts. "Total vulnerability." He looked at me, truly looked. Not with assessing eyes now, but with the raw openness I had glimpsed in moments of shared danger. At the pulse beating faintly at the base of my throat, the slight flush on my high cheekbones, the way I met his gaze without flinching. This depth of merging... it wasn't just technical; it felt profound, echoing something ancient within his culture, within us.

"This requires absolute synchronization, Keket. Shared focus. An anchor."

Anchor. The word echoed, resonating with the memory of his hand in mine during the chaotic first surge, the explosion, the subsequent controlled flash, the terrifying intimacy. My gaze flickered to his hand, then quickly away, focusing on the technical setup, the equipment we would use. This physical contact wasn't impulse today; it was methodology, a hypothesis based on our previous chaotic interactions, a shared circuit requiring trust, proximity, vulnerability. My scientific mind embraced the logic, the elegant simplicity of the potential solution; the woman recoiled slightly from the dangerous intimacy it demanded, the memory of being overwhelmed still fresh. Yet, the drive to understand, to map this impossible frontier, was stronger than my apprehension. This was discovery on a scale I'd never dreamed of, a purpose far removed from optimizing corporate extraction routes. This felt... meaningful, vital, a chance to understand something truly profound that might hold the key to Xylos's survival and the Path itself. A chance that felt increasingly urgent with the Collective looming and the Scarabite-7 draining.

"We learned yesterday," I stated, meeting his gaze, pushing down the tremor of apprehension by focusing on the data, on the science, "Physical contact, shared focus, proximity to the resonant crystal. It stabilizes the connection, channels the energy. My bio-filaments, your connection to the Heartstone – they act as the necessary circuit." I checked the readings on the small console I'd brought in, calibrating the regulators, ensuring the safety overrides were active.

Zephyr nodded solemnly, confirming my analysis, a collaborative partner in this scientific endeavor. "Two resonant points," he agreed. "Your amplified Watcher senses acting as the lens, calibrated to perceive the Path's currents, my connection to the Heartstone as the source, the anchor, the power. We attempt to guide the flow, not simply be swept away." He stepped closer, the air crackling with latent energy between us, the hum of the Scarabite-7 spire intensifying. He extended his hand, palm up, a silent offering of trust and shared risk, his fingers long and strong, the patterns on his skin pulsing faintly in response to the crystal's energy, mirroring the faint glow beneath my own skin. Taking a deep breath that tasted of ozone and energized crystal and the unique, grounding scent of him, I met his gaze and placed my hand in his, my fingers closing around his, the warmth of his skin a sudden, sharp sensation that felt both alien and undeniably right.

Keket and Zephyr:

No explosion. This time, the connection surged, powerful, undeniable, but channeled, guided by intent and the carefully calibrated tech. It flowed like a warm, electric river, humming through their joined hands, amplified by the immense Scarabite-7 spire vibrating beside them, its emerald light intensifying.

The tingling sensation intensified, spreading up their arms, weaving their distinct energies – Keket's focused starlight amplified by tech, Zephyr's deep planetary resonance – into a stable, harmonic circuit. The low hum in the chamber deepened, coalescing into an almost audible tone, pure and resonant, a single, powerful chord that felt like the true voice of Xylos. They were linked – mind to mind, energy to energy, anchored by touch and intent, by Terran technology and Kryll biology, by shared purpose and unspoken connection forged in crisis and growing intimacy. The physical contact wasn't just about energy transfer; it was about vulnerability, about yielding control, about a trust that had grown between them, amplifying the resonance, deepening the channel.

Keket:

Focus, I thought, anchoring myself in the steady warmth of his hand, in the familiar hum of my bio-filaments aligning with his energy. Grounding. Guiding. I consciously shaped the flow, offering a specific memory, something imbued with purpose and the drive that defined me. See this. Understand the yearning. The reason I seek the stars. The sterile hub, the endless data streams, the view of Earth from orbit, the feeling of being trapped in a gilded cage, the promise of the Sanction, the hope for something better. The 'ground static' I fled, replaced by this terrifying, exhilarating current.

Zephyr:

Her mind opened to mine, a landscape of sharp intelligence, fierce loyalty, and that core of restless fire. The sterile grey of her metal world, the endless starfield beckoning outside a viewport – I felt the familiar cage of its walls and her restless spirit yearning, aching, for the dark beyond, for the purpose she hadn't yet found. It was the freedom I'd unconsciously craved, a universe away from my grounded duty, and it resonated with an ache I rarely allowed myself to feel. The shared glimpse of her inner world deepened the protectiveness, the undeniable pull.

Keket and Zephyr:

The chamber shimmered, resolving into clarity, not into a memory, but into a new reality. We weren't flung into chaos; we entered. Luminous currents flowed around our shared consciousness, vast, powerful, but navigable. We perceived the energy streams, the complex network branching into infinities, anchored yet free, guided by our combined will and calibrated perception.

This felt like true flight, the transcendence Keket yearned for. Together, we focused our combined will, directing the stable energy into the Nexus Path. We weren't flung into chaos; we entered. Luminous currents flowed around our shared consciousness, vast, powerful, but navigable. We perceived the energy streams, the complex network branching into infinities, anchored yet free. We had woven Kryll intuition and Terran technology into a bridge across realities.

The following explorations were transcendence. Anchored to Xylos, we soared.

Zephyr:

I saw the Serpentis Nebula not as data, but as breathtaking, swirling cosmic dust, feeling the raw energy of creation Keket had described with such longing. Keket guided us through the profound, silent beauty between stars, brushed our awareness against worlds teeming with unimaginable life, her awe and wonder amplified and shared through our bond. She shared her past – Earth from orbit, the cold grandeur of stations – letting me feel her history, her drive to escape the 'static' for something real. It was the freedom I'd unconsciously craved, realized through her eyes, made tangible through our connection. Within the Path, communication was seamless thought, shared sensation, the bond a conduit, not a chain. Trust, deep and unspoken, solidified star by star, forged in shared vulnerability and cosmic awe. Emerging from the Path, the chamber felt both alien and intimately familiar. Keket looked at me, truly seeing him not just as a Kryll leader or a figure of intense attraction, but as the being whose loneliness had mirrored her own in the void, whose fierce pride for his dying world now felt like a wound in her own heart. He, in turn, saw not just a Terran captain, but the woman who carried the restless fire of stars within her, whose yearning for purpose resonated with a hidden part of his own soul. The raw intimacy of the Path had stripped away all pretense, leaving a bond forged in shared cosmic awe and the terrifying beauty of seeing another's true self

We were partners, charting the infinite, our individual drives harmonizing in this impossible space. The subtle, unsettling hum beneath the city seemed to fade here, replaced by the silent, immense potential of the Path itself.

Keket:

This current felt different. Older. Deeper. A subtle shift in the energy flow, a frequency that resonated not with cosmic dust or planetary hums, but with something... ancient. We pushed into uncharted Nexus territory, the energy thick with the dust of forgotten epochs, guided by an instinct that went beyond calibration or lore. The unsettling visions from earlier, the whispers of screaming shadows, seemed tied to this deeper current.

Then, we sensed it – colossal, woven from the Path's fabric, a geometry that fractured Terran understanding. A vast, intricate structure of energy and information, anchored somewhere deep within the cosmic currents. And the energy flowing through our bond, channeling the Heartstone's power amplified by my tech, felt like a filament connecting us directly to its impossible scale. As our awareness neared, it... noticed. Noticed us. The realization sent a jolt of pure terror through the shared space of our minds. We weren't just travelers; we were perceived. Pure conceptual data flooded our minds – non-linear, overwhelming – galactic memory compressed into instants, layered with abstract warnings and questions that defied translation. The Nexus Path wasn't just transit; it was aware. Ancient. Vast.

And within that flood, a specific resonance focused, probing our unique, bonded frequency – human tech amplifying Kryll sense, Terran innovation woven with Kryll intuition, powered by Xylos's heart. Recognition? Curiosity? An echo of Nana's whispers about sensing the unseen currents, amplified to a cosmic scale. A silent query: What are you? This harmony... is new. Our bond, the unintended consequence of Keket's tech and Zephyr's heritage interacting, amplified by shared risk and earned intimacy, was a key, interacting with this primal awareness in a way never before possible, drawing its attention.

We recoiled, snapping back to the chamber, the mundane world jarring after the cosmic ocean, the return to solid reality almost painful in its abruptness. My heart hammered against my ribs, a frantic counterpoint to the residual hum of the Scarabite-7. I met Zephyr's wide, luminous eyes – shock, awe, fear mirroring my own. The mistrust felt centuries past, irrelevant in the face of this new, shared reality forged in cosmic fire and profound, terrifying intimacy. The universe had cracked open, revealing infinities, and we had just been acknowledged by something that resided within them. Our bond wasn't just biology or technology; it was a key to galactic secrets, held by ancient sentience within the Path. Our journey hadn't ended; it had exploded onto a cosmic scale, our carefully planned mission dwarfed by this cosmic encounter. This, I realized with chilling certainty, was the true conflict. The Collective,

Faction Twelve, the Scarabite-7 drain – they were pieces on a board I hadn't even known existed until this moment.

Keket and Zephyr:

Back in the chamber, the Path's echo slowly subsided, leaving a vibrating silence charged with the weight of their discovery. "Zephyr," Keket breathed, her voice raw with the aftermath, "if the Path is aware... what now?"

He met her gaze, awe tempered by ancestral caution. The warnings in the ancient texts about 'Silent Watchers Beyond' resonated with terrifying clarity. "It means the stakes dwarf the Collective's ambitions," he stated, his voice low but resolute, the Protector facing a threat beyond any historical record. "Control of this Path... it's not about faster ships. It's knowledge. Power. Realities reshaped. And whatever that was... it noticed us." He gestured to her star charts, now feeling impossibly small, remnants of a universe that was far more complex and alive than they had ever imagined. "And we, Keket – this unexpected harmony between Terran and Kryll – we knocked, and something answered. We hold a key." His voice was low, filled with the weight of universes, the burden of this new, cosmic secret settling heavily upon them both.

"But to what door?" Keket whispered, voicing the terrifying uncertainty, her mind, the scientist's mind, grappling with concepts that defied all known physics. "And what waits on the other side?"

The question hung between them, echoing in the quiet chamber, terrifying and magnificent. The Scarabite-7 drain, the Collective threat, the internal dissent – these were still urgent problems, but they were now framed within a context of cosmic sentience and unimaginable power. Their bond, once a source of confusion and personal tension, was now revealed as the catalyst for this interaction, the key to a path that could lead to salvation or destruction. The next steps were unknown, unmapped, and more perilous than ever. The ultimate conflict wasn't external resource war or internal political strife; it was the struggle to understand and navigate a universe that was profoundly, terrifyingly, alive, and that now knew they existed.

Chapter 19: Entering the Uncharted Akhet – A Harmony of Souls

Keket

The air in the Resonance Chamber was no longer just charged; it *lived*. It pulsed. It sang with a frantic, beautiful energy that vibrated through my very core, resonating with the Ashe flowing through my veins, amplified by the bio-filaments woven beneath my skin. Immediately following the raw, terrifying revelation of the Aware Path, the shared glimpse of the Neteru's vast consciousness, the terrifying sense of being noticed – the chamber transformed entirely. It was less a room, more a perceived threshold, a place where the veil between mundane physical reality and the Akhet – the cosmic spirit world, the vibrant, terrifying horizon where worlds met and consciousness flowed – felt impossibly thin, porous, almost transparent to the raw magic on the other side. The crystal walls, moments ago merely architecture, now pulsed with colors that defied my earthly vision – shifting spectrums of light, shades of emerald, amethyst, and gold that twisted and folded in on themselves, painting abstract, three-dimensional patterns directly onto my perception, patterns that seemed to echo the intricate designs of my bio-filaments, of the tattoos on my skin, of Zephyr's own glowing marks. Sounds didn't reach my ears conventionally; they resonated directly in my bones, in the space between heartbeats, a symphony of felt vibrations, whispers of cosmic song, of creation and dissolution, that both awed and terrified in their unpredictable shifts. The geometry of the space seemed to breathe, solid lines of crystal warping and flowing like liquid light, the very architecture of the chamber alive with a raw, untamed Ashe (life force/power) that swirled visibly in the air, coalescing into ephemeral shapes, reaching out, reacting to our presence, to *us*, with a palpable, magical intensity.

Here and there, embedded in the flowing crystal architecture or perhaps manifesting directly from the intensified Ashe, appeared clusters of gemstones. They looked like precious jewels from old Earth lore – some clear and sparkling like the finest diamonds, others glowing with the deep red of rubies, the vibrant blue of sapphires, or the lush green of emeralds, but clearly of unearthly origin. They pulsed with their own subtle light, drawing the eye, beckoning touch.

We stood in the epicenter of this transformation, Zephyr and I, mere meters apart. But the distance felt negligible, a polite fiction in the face of the overwhelming reality of our bond. My senses, amplified by my Watcher heritage and calibrated tech, felt overwhelmed, struggling to process the sheer volume of impossible, magical data. But my bond with Zephyr, the connection forged in crisis and cemented in terrifying intimacy, became not just an anchor, but a volatile, unpredictable engine fueled by our shared Ashe.

The proximity alone was a catalyst, turning the chamber into a canvas for raw, unpredictable magic. Bursts of wild Ashe, raw and unpredictable, arced between us – not electricity, but shimmering, living light that seemed to pulse with the frantic, powerful beat of *our* hearts, with the raw energy of our connection, of our burgeoning love. It triggered intense, spontaneous magical phenomena in the immediate environment, phenomena that felt tied to the raw, untamed energy of our combined connection. A crystal structure near Zephyr pulsed violently, not just with light, but with internal energy, briefly dissolving into a cascade of what looked like liquid starlight before snapping back into its solid form with a resonant chime that vibrated through the floor, a sound I felt reflected in my own chest, a counterpoint to the frantic beat of my heart. A patch of the crystal floor near my boots felt gravity warp, pushing downward with impossible force before snapping back, leaving my balance momentarily askew, a physical echo of the way he anchored me, of the trust I placed in his presence. Echoes of ancient sounds, like distant chanting that resonated with Nana's tales of priestesses weaving cosmic harmonies, or the crash of unseen waves on impossible shores, resonated from the air itself, seeming to swirl *around* us, *because* of us. A sudden, brief appearance of fantastical flora, glowing with impossible internal light and singing a silent, felt melody, sprouted from a seam in the wall, only to wither and vanish moments later, leaving behind a faint, sweet, magical scent of Ashe that felt strangely like the air after his kiss in. This was the raw magic our bond unleashed, unpredictable and potent, just by existing close together in this charged threshold space, a physical manifestation of the energy swirling between our souls, a testament to the power of our connection.

Amidst this chaotic surge of external magic, something even more profound, more intimately terrifying, erupted *between* us, within the shared space our bond created. The cosmic echoes of the Neteru's gaze from Chapter

18 intensified, filtering directly through our shared connection, bypassing my conventional senses entirely. Surges of pure concept, impossible to translate into words, washed over me – not thoughts, but raw data of immense, indifferent consciousnesses. Glimpses of impossible, non-physical forms flickered at the edges of my vision, woven from cosmic light and raw Ashe, reflecting ancient, immense consciousnesses that defied understanding, their presence a felt pressure in the air around us, a sense of being observed by something vast and ancient. These came and went without warning, dictated by the unpredictable currents of the Akhet pressing in, but also, I suspected, amplified by the raw, untamed Ashe our bond was generating.

And interwoven with these cosmic echoes, a new, chaotic wave of sensory data flooded my mind – Zephyr's raw thoughts. Not processed, not filtered, just the unfiltered torrent of his inner world, accessible now, overwhelming in its honesty and vulnerability.

Fear... deep, primal... like the Unraveling... Xylos... bleeding... for you... never let go...

Awe... breathtaking beauty... terrifying power... can't look away... pulled in... together... with you... always...

Protect... must shield... my Ashe... your light... dangerous... this power... ours... Ma'at... guide us... need you... more than Ashe...

His emotions, fragmented concepts, primal fears, hidden desires, unfiltered reactions, a current of intense protectiveness and undeniable love – all crashing into my consciousness. Chaotic. Involuntary. Disorienting. A layer of intense, dizzying, terrifying intimacy layered atop the cosmic awe and terror. My own thoughts, a torrent of frantic scientific analysis warring with intuitive understanding, Watcher heritage clashing with sheer fear, and a surge of profound love for him, for Xylos, for this terrifying, beautiful magic, surged back at him, equally unfiltered. This was telepathy. Hearing each other's raw minds, a chaotic, unpredictable, yet undeniably profound consequence of our bond's amplification in this magical threshold. Every fear for him, every flicker of hope, every ounce of attraction, every beat of my heart was laid bare between us. To hear his raw fear for Xylos, to feel the crushing weight of his protectiveness not just for his people but intensely, overwhelmingly, for .me, was shattering. And for Zephyr, to be buffeted by my pragmatic terror, her desperate need to analyze and understand this wild magic, yet beneath it all, the fierce, unwavering pulse of her loyalty and a love so new and bright it seared through his defenses... It was agony and ecstasy. This unfiltered honesty, this complete baring of souls, was more terrifying than any cosmic entity, and more profoundly binding than any spoken vow. In that chaotic shared space, where only truth existed, their love wasn't just a feeling; it became the very fabric of their sanity.

<Analyze! Systems nominal? No, they're not! What is this Ashe? How... Nana? Was this... the Veil? Akhet... open? With us? My Zephyr... his fear...> My thoughts a desperate search for understanding, a fight against being utterly overwhelmed, a fierce protective current flowing towards him.

< The drain... Scarabite... faster? No... just the echoes... hold to me, Keket! Hold to our harmony... control... this power... Isfet... pushing through... the wound... it calls...> His thought was a point of desperate focus, a plea to our connection as an anchor against the rising chaos, a raw need for my presence.

<He's scared... truly scared... not just Commander... my love... with me... always... The Collective... so far... Faction Twelve... close... ripples of discord... Isfet... rising... but we are here... together... stronger...> My thought acknowledging the abstract threats, but emphasizing the tangible reality of *us*, our shared presence and fight, the undeniable strength of our combined Ashe.

Struggling with the overwhelming influx, the chaotic telepathy and cosmic input, the sheer unpredictability of the magic exploding around us, we instinctively reached for a different kind of connection. Not words spoken aloud, which felt impossible here. Not the chaotic flood of raw thoughts. A focus. An intention. Weaving our combined Ashe, guided by a desperate, shared need for clarity and control, but also by a powerful, magnetic pull towards each other. I felt Zephyr's will joining mine, a familiar resonance from the controlled test, but amplified, magical, demanding every ounce of our combined focus, every fiber of our being, every beat of our interconnected hearts. Describe the effort as a conscious weaving of light and will in our shared mental space, a dance of intention, a desperate, beautiful attempt to create a pocket of Ma'at within the surrounding Isfet. And it worked. The chaos of raw thoughts subsided slightly, replaced by a channel. Mind-speak. Not just words, but shared feelings, images, and intuitive understanding woven together by our bond's intense energy. A new language born of our shared journey, our love, and our burgeoning magical power. A language of soul speaking to soul, a language of Ashe flowing between us.

<*Keket. Can you... find Ma'at... here... with me?*> Zephyr's presence in my mind was clearer now, focused, a point of stability in the swirling magic. His thought carried a wave of desperate hope, a plea for balance, a deep need for my presence beside him.

<*Anchor... with you... always... my love... The Ashe... so wild... beautiful... and terrifying... Isfet... strong... but our harmony... stronger... The drain... it aches...*> My mind-speak conveyed the sense of being pulled in multiple directions, the magical wound on Xylos felt as a constant ache, but overshadowed by the undeniable strength and love of our bond.

<*The threats... Isfet... yes... but small... ripples... compared to this...*> Zephyr's thought shifted focus, acknowledging the abstract threats but highlighting the new, overwhelming scale of the cosmic reality they faced, a thought interwoven with awe and protectiveness. <*The Akhet... calls... a current... unpredictable... but... it is the Path... ours... together...*>

<*Not strategy... no map...*> my thought echoed his, releasing the need for control, for understanding in logical terms, replaced by a profound trust in the magical flow and in him. <*Trust the current... trust us... my love...*> a surge of terrifying faith in our bond, in our combined Ashe.

<*Yes... trust us...*> his thought resonated, a wave of profound relief, love, and determination.

<*Our love... that is the true Ma'at... the anchor...*> My thought pulsed, clarity blooming amidst the Akhet's chaos. <It weaves us... it guides us... together... my heart...> His mental presence solidified beside mine, a steady light in the cosmic storm.

<*We are the balance... together...*>.

My gaze fell upon a cluster of the magical gemstones embedded in the swirling crystal near us. They shimmered, reflecting the chaotic, beautiful Ashe arcing between Zephyr and me. One, a deep sapphire blue, seemed to pulse with a felt sense of ancient knowledge. Another, ruby red, vibrated with passion and danger. A clear, diamond-like stone radiated pure, chaotic energy. Drawn by instinct, by a pull from the stone and a shared curiosity felt through mind-speak, I reached out, my fingers brushing the cool, smooth surface of the sapphire-like gem.

A sudden surge of feeling. Not just energy, but emotion, ancient and vast, flowed into my consciousness through my touch and our bond. Wisdom. Patience. A deep, sorrowful understanding of time and consequence. Zephyr felt it too, a wave of shared sensation and knowledge washing over both of us.

<The stones... they hold... memory... Ashe...> his thought resonated, wondering mingling with caution.

He reached out, his own scaled fingers touching the ruby-like stone. A burst of fierce, protective love, of territoriality, of ancient anger, flowed into our shared perception. Danger. Passion. A warning.

<They feel...> my thought sent back, overwhelmed. *<Feelings... power...>*

<Echoes...> his thought confirmed. *<Of Ashe... trapped... from the Akhet... from Neteru...>*

The stones were fragments of the Akhet, holding echoes of the cosmic forces and the ancient history woven into its currents. Unpredictable. Revealing.

<The current...> Zephyr's thought refocused us, the pull of the pathway intensifying. *<It is opening... now...>*

The step into the Akhet was not a calculated plan based on threats or logic. It was triggered by this overwhelming, unpredictable magical event. A sudden surge of our combined Ashe, reacting to a chaotic Akhet current and perhaps amplified by the energy of the gemstones, ripped open a temporary, unstable pathway directly before us – a shimmering, non-physical vortex swirling with impossible colors, resonating with the felt cosmic song, pulsing with the undeniable pull of the Neteru's echoes, beckoning us forward. A specific Neteru's powerful echo became an irresistible, silent pull in our minds, amplified by our bond, compelling us forward with a force that defied resistance. Or perhaps the threshold space itself, unable to contain the raw Ashe our bond was unleashing and the pull of the Akhet, collapsed, forcing us into the magical realm. Our choice wasn't strategy; it was a shared, instinctive surrender to this mystical compulsion, a leap of faith guided by the undeniable pull of the magic, by the sense that this unpredictable current was the only way forward, and that we could only face it together.

<Ready? My love...> Zephyr's thought, a wave of fierce resolve, protectiveness, and profound trust and love that resonated through our linked

Ashe, a question that asked everything and nothing, a promise whispered soul-to-soul.

<*With you... always... my heart...*> my own, a surrender to the current, to the magic, to him, a terrifying and exhilarating leap into the unknown, into our shared destiny.

Hands clasped, their Ashe intertwining, their minds linked, their hearts beating as one, they stepped across the threshold. Swept into the vibrant, unpredictable, magical realm of the Akhet. The sensation of conventional reality dissolving was surreal, overwhelming, a beautiful, terrifying dissolution. Colors became sounds, forms became concepts, the feeling of stepping into a realm of pure magic and unexpected, fluid forms, together. The final image is them being pulled into the unknown, their hands clasped, their bond's Ashe a single point of intensifying, chaotic-yet-harmonious light, a beacon of love in the swirling cosmic currents of the Akhet, the echoes of the Neteru receding for a moment as they plunged deeper into the magical flow, together.

Chapter 20: Navigating the Cosmic Flow of Ashe

Keket

The plunge was breathtaking. Terrifying. Immediately following that shared leap across the unpredictable threshold, conventional reality didn't just dissolve; it ceased to hold meaning. We were immersed. Fully. In the Akhet. This realm was a constantly shifting landscape woven from pure, vibrant Ashe and cosmic energy. It defied every physical law, every navigational chart I'd ever known. Forms were fluid, made of light and concept – mountains of solidified thought rising and falling like waves, rivers of flowing Ashe carrying echoes of creation, structures that rearranged themselves as my consciousness, amplified by our bond, perceived them. Gravity, up or down, past or future were meaningless here; direction was a feeling, a resonance within the flow. The air, or what passed for it, was a symphony of felt vibrations and abstract colors that sang directly to my soul, a language of pure magic.

Our movement was dictated entirely by the unpredictable flow of the Akhet's currents. We were not piloting, not traveling in any conventional sense; we were being swept along, sometimes gently floating through vast, silent realms of pure creation energy that felt like stepping into the heart of a newborn star, filled with the promise of potential. Other times, we were violently tossed by turbulent eddies of Isfet (chaos), dark, gnawing currents that clawed at our harmony, threatening to unravel our very forms. We navigated intuitively, guided by the constant, bright resonance of our bond – our shared Ashe – and sudden flashes of insight felt directly in our minds.

<Hold to me, my heart! The current... it pulls...> Zephyr's thought resonated, a wave of fierce resolve and trust cutting through the disorientation, his presence a steady beacon in the chaos.

<With you! Our Ashe... our light... together...> my thought pulsed back, focusing my will, feeling our combined energy surge, a tangible rope of light connecting us, pulling us through the turmoil. We had to learn to read these magical currents using our combined Ashe sensitivity – sensing the flow of pure Ashe as warm, bright rivers of well-being and power, the presence of Isfet as

cold, discordant turbulence that threatened to shatter our focus, the pull of Neteru as resonant frequencies that drew us towards profound encounters.

We encountered manifestations of the Neteru (cosmic forces/beings) and other magical entities within the Akhet. These encounters were unpredictable, surreal. Not planned meetings, but sudden appearances as we drifted through the currents, dictated by the flow and the resonance of our bond. A sentient storm of starlight might coalesce before us, singing songs of cosmic law (Ma'at) directly into our minds, testing our understanding of universal balance. A living pattern of consciousness woven into the Ashe flow might appear, vast and ancient, embodying a cosmic principle like Creation or Destruction, presenting us with profound, non-linear insights felt as sudden, undeniable truths. We saw echoes of ancient magical battles fought in epochs past, perceived as flashes of raw, clashing Ashe in the distance. These interactions were mystical tests or exchanges, not battles as I knew them, often presenting us with profound, non-linear insights or challenges related to balance, harmony, or the very nature of Ashe itself. The entities were specifically intrigued by or reactive to the unique harmony and intensity of our combined Ashe, a new, unexpected phenomenon in the Akhet's ancient flow. Our love, our trust, amplified our Ashe, making us visible, making us significant, drawing the attention of cosmic forces.

The challenges they faced were magical and unpredictable, directly testing the core of our bond. We stumbled upon a section of the Akhet where Isfet was overwhelming, a vortex of unraveling reality, a place where Ma'at struggled to hold. We had to use the pure harmony (Ma'at) of our bond, the combined strength of our Ashe, focusing our shared will, to create a small pocket of stability, a shimmering bubble of order in the surrounding chaos, preventing the Isfet from consuming us. We encountered a point of depleted Ashe, a cosmic wound in the Akhet's flow, and felt compelled to channel our own combined energy to revitalize it, temporarily, feeling our own Ashe flow outwards like a healing balm, a shared sacrifice that strengthened the current. Or a Neteru, manifesting as a living constellation of brilliant Ashe, presented a mystical riddle felt directly in our minds about the balance of life and death, creation and destruction (Khepri's cycle), a riddle only our combined intuition and understanding of cosmic truth, filtered through our bond's unique resonance, could solve. Our teamwork was a dance of weaving our Ashe together, our minds linked, our hearts beating as one, creating small, vital pockets of Ma'at within the Akhet's overwhelming, beautiful chaos.

The "resolution" of our journey wasn't achieving a specific strategic goal; it was causing a significant, unpredictable magical change in the Akhet or its connection to Xylos/reality as a consequence of our journey and the power of our bond. As we navigated a particularly turbulent current tied to the Scarabite-7 drain – felt as a raw, aching wound in the Akhet's flow, a place where Xylos's Ashe was being siphoned – we channeled our combined Ashe, weaving a complex pattern of harmony (Ma'at) and intention into the chaotic energy. This wasn't a cure, not a permanent fix to the drain, but it caused a significant, unpredictable magical change. It temporarily altered the flow of that specific Akhet current of Ashe, redirecting its most destructive, consuming aspects away from Xylos, creating a momentary ease in the ache of the drain, a temporary restoration of balance achieved through the sheer force of our bond's magic.

We were suddenly back. The intense magical state receded, the overwhelming sensory input resolving back into the familiar (now subtly transformed) Resonance Chamber. We stood together, hands still clasped, fundamentally changed and bound even tighter. The Akhet's vibrant energies lingered, a felt presence beneath the crystal walls, but the terrifying unpredictability had lessened, replaced by a sense of profound, earned peace. The HFN scene. Exhausted, muscles aching with the strain of wielding such power, but alive. Our bond was a vibrant, visible light flowing between us, a source of profound magical harmony (Ma'at) in a universe that was now known to be filled with powerful, beautiful chaos (Isfet). Our love was not just emotional; it was a source of powerful, creative Ashe, our partnership a living act of creating balance in the cosmos.

<We...> Zephyr's thought resonated, raw, filled with wonder and exhaustion, a simple acknowledgment of the impossible journey shared.

<We did it... for now...> my thought finished, acknowledging the temporary nature of the change, the vastness of what remained, the weight of the secret we carried.

Dialogue flowed, mind-to-mind, a seamless exchange of thought and feeling, focusing on the depth of our connection, the terrifying beauty of the magic we experienced, and our shared purpose rooted in our bond. We spoke of the Neteru we sensed, the currents we navigated, the fragile balance we briefly restored. We were together, committed, drawing strength from our combined Ashe, our hands still clasped, grounding us in reality. Later, in the quiet stillness of the spire, long after the echoes of the Akhet had subsided, Zephyr turned to me. The new light in his eyes, the visible thrum of Ashe beneath his skin, mirrored her own transformation. He raised their still-clasped hands, his thumb brushing the back of hers where her own bio-filaments glowed faintly. 'The universe knows us now, Keket,' he murmured, his voice raw with the awe of their journey. 'Not as Kryll and Terran, but as... one resonance.' I leaned into him, finding solace in his solid warmth. 'And we know ourselves, Zephyr,' I whispered, 'and what we are together.' Their foreheads touched, a silent communion of two souls irrevocably altered, their love not just a personal solace, but a nascent cosmic force, a beacon against the beautiful, terrifying chaos they had faced, and would face again.

Miles away, on a dust-choked mining colony orbiting a red dwarf star, a weary prospector with hands calloused by ore felt a sudden, inexplicable surge of vibrant energy bloom in his chest – a warmth unlike the sterile heat of the habs, a feeling of *life*, of potent Ashe. His eyes, scanning the barren rock, flickered to a patch of dust where impossible flora, glowing with internal Ashe, spontaneously blossomed for a fleeting second, singing a silent, felt song. He reached out a trembling hand, drawn by an instinct he couldn't explain, his dormant Ashe awakening with a jolt. He felt a sudden, inexplicable pull towards the stars, towards a destiny he never imagined.

Across the galaxy, on a bustling trade station, a sharp-eyed information broker, sifting through encrypted transmissions, suddenly perceived a pattern in the data feed that wasn't just code – a fleeting, complex wave of Ashe, carrying echoes of cosmic song and ancient warnings. Her implant flagged it as an anomaly, but her mind, sensitive in ways she never understood, felt a powerful pull, a resonance with this strange, living data from a quadrant she barely knew existed. It felt like a message, a key, drawing her into a mystery tied to forces beyond her comprehension.

Deep within the rigid hierarchy of a Collective research vessel, a young xenobotanist studying ancient life forms from forgotten worlds, felt a sudden, violent surge of Ashe from a secured artifact from an age long past – a magical echo of the unpredictable currents navigated by Keket and Zephyr. The artifact, inert for centuries, pulsed with light, its form briefly shifting before stabilizing, leaving the scientist reeling, questioning everything she thought she knew about biological and energetic life. This anomaly felt tied to something vast, something new, something dangerous she had to understand, pulling her research in an unexpected direction.

Back on Xylos, Keket and Zephyr, visibly marked by their journey (a new light in their eyes, a subtle, felt Ashe glow beneath their skin, their signatures now visibly intertwined), stood together. Their hands were clasped, their combined Ashe a vibrant, palpable light flowing between them, a living force, a testament to their journey into the Akhet. They were the guardians not just of Xylos, but of a specific current or aspect of the Akhet they now understood or were responsible for. The conventional threats (Collective, Faction Twelve) were mentioned as distant echoes, pale compared to the vast, unpredictable magical cosmos they had just touched. Their bond was the core of their power and destiny. The final words emphasize their HFN – "Their harmony, a beacon in the endless flow of Ashe, a promise against the encroaching Isfet" – and the sense of being irrevocably tied to the beautiful, terrifying, unpredictable magical unknown, together, ready for the next wave of the series, ready to navigate the cosmic currents and strive for balance in a universe of chaos.

Don't miss out!

Visit the website below and you can sign up to receive emails whenever Lyra Xolani publishes a new book. There's no charge and no obligation.

https://books2read.com/r/B-A-EKFVD-DQXHG

BOOKS 2 READ

Connecting independent readers to independent writers.

About the Author

From the grounding currents of Maryland, Lyra Xolani navigates the boundless Akhet of imagination, ever creating. A weaver of cosmic tapestries, they blend starlight and ancient Ashe into tales of impossible connections, navigating chaotic realities alongside unforgettable characters. Living surrounded by family, they find the profound resonance that fuels journeys beyond the stars.

Read more at LyraXolani.com.

www.ingramcontent.com/pod-product-compliance
Lightning Source LLC
Chambersburg PA
CBHW030347180626
46812CB00007B/2796